"That's all it was, Ginny. Just a kiss."

Steel paused and then continued, "You didn't seem to object the other night."

"When I was too exhausted and miserable to care what happened to me?" she said acidly. "You found that encouraging?"

"Intriguing." A narrow smile turned the corners of his mouth—that warm, exciting mouth that had so recently laid claim to her own. "I wondered if you respond so warmly to your fiancé's attentions...."

Angela Wells was educated in a convent in Essex,
England, and later left the bustling world of media
marketing and advertising to marry and start a family
in a suburb of London. Writing started out as a hobby,
and she uses backgrounds she knows well from her
many travels, especially in the Mediterranean area.
Her ambition, she says , in addition to writing many
more romances, is to spend more time in Australia—
especially Sydney and the islands of the Great
Barrier Reef.

Books by Angela Wells

Dishonourable Seduction
Angela Wells

Harlequin Books

TORONTO • NEW YORK • LONDON
AMSTERDAM • PARIS • SYDNEY • HAMBURG
STOCKHOLM • ATHENS • TOKYO • MILAN
MADRID • WARSAW • BUDAPEST • AUCKLAND

ISBN 0-373-17267-2

DISHONOURABLE SEDUCTION

First North American Publication 1996.

Copyright © 1995 by Angela Wells.

This edition published by arrangement with Harlequin Books S.A.

® and ™ are trademarks of the publisher. Trademarks indicated with
® are registered in the United States Patent and Trademark Office, the
Canadian Trade Marks Office and in other countries.

Printed in U.S.A.

CHAPTER ONE

'WHAT the devil do you think you're doing?'

The angry male voice broke into Ginny's reverie as the door of her office burst open as if before the blast of a hurricane. Jumping to her feet with an instinctive yelp of fright, she pivoted away from her desk to confront the intruder.

Her eyes registered a man probably in his early thirties: dark, short, curly hair, oval countenance with broad forehead, high cheekbones, rounded chin and straight, strong nose. Painfully aware that she was alone in the small office isolated at one side of the large yard outside Sullivan's storage sheds, a sense of self-preservation urged her to file away in her mind details of the intruder. In normal circumstances, he would have been more than passingly attractive, she realised distractedly, but clearly the situation was far from normal because the generous-lipped mouth was held in a tight line and the dark eyes glowered at her from beneath black horizontal brows with uncompromising hostility.

Still intent on documenting his appearance lest at some later date she might be called upon to provide it to the police, she dragged her eyes, grey as a winter sky, from his angry expression, drifting them downwards to encompass handmade leather shoes, before returning via long male legs elegantly clad in peat-coloured trousers, the soft finish and tailoring of which suggested they were made of silk, attached to a lean body, formally clothed in a tailored shirt with knotted silk tie and topped by a natural-coloured linen jacket.

Not the uniform of a thug. On the other hand not the kind of clothes worn by a man of modest means. The thought Mafia entered her mind only to be dismissed immediately as fanciful, despite the fact that every muscle and tendon of the man's long body was primed for aggression, the threat substantiated by the expression on his face. Sullivan's was a small, suburban-based company, not one likely to attract the attention of the mob. Nevertheless her initial anxiety deepened.

Why on earth hadn't she closed the office down and left with the rest of the small office staff at five-thirty? she wondered silently. It wasn't as if she'd spent the extra time profitably. In fact all she'd done since their departure was to dwell on the increasing problems facing her father's company without having been able to find any dynamic solution to them.

Now she was faced with getting rid of this hostile caller before she could lock up and go home. All her senses told her she was going to have her work cut out to engage him in civil conversation, let alone persuade him to remove his disquieting masculine bulk from her father's premises!

'Can I help you?' From somewhere she dredged up a voice of commendable calmness, forcing herself to scan the belligerent face confronting her with an impersonal smile. Perhaps he'd made a mistake and his business wasn't with her after all, she thought optimistically.

'Where is Leo Sullivan?' The voice which emerged from the strong, lightly tanned throat was deep, slightly accented. A surface smoothness disguised a rough undertone of anger. Honey on toasted waffles. Beneath black brows drawn into a frown, vengeful eyes took their toll on her. Ginny's heart sank in recognition that her wishful thinking had been just that—wishful!

'I'm sorry my father's not available,' she returned firmly, banishing from her mind the cruel image of Leo Sullivan as she had last seen him, pale and emaciated in a hospital bed. 'For the time being, I'm in charge.' With an effort she disciplined her voice to assume an authority she was far from feeling. 'However, we're closed for tonight. We open again at nine tomorrow. If you'd like to come back then——'

'I've come for my order. Campsis vine, scarlet canna, two pomegranate trees and twenty-five floral table decorations.' He interrupted her reply as if it had as little relevance to the conversation as the state of the weather, continuing in evenly paced words as if speaking to a child, and not a very bright one at that, 'My dear Miss Sullivan, bare walls and alcoves are not part of the new décor for the Keys of Corfu. More importantly, unless I take back the floral table posies, with their integral lights, the restaurant will remain shut tonight. It may surprise you, but our customers actually like to see what they're eating!'

His laboured, patronising tone did nothing to quieten Ginny's discomfort. In fact it added to her disquiet, as did the mention of the restaurant's name. A spasm of alarm raised the small hairs on the back of her graceful neck.

Unthinkingly, she pushed her tumble of tawny-coloured hair away from her face, anchoring it behind her small neat ears, in a gesture which betrayed her uneasiness. Drat! Silently she cursed her earlier impetuosity. It seemed Duncan had been right after all, and her dynamic plan devised to drag Sullivan's from near bankruptcy into profitable trading had already back-fired on her. Her father's bookkeeper had warned her that an arbitrary change of business procedure from monthly terms of payment to cash on delivery would only exacerbate Sullivan's problems.

Perhaps she *had* acted too hastily in insisting that Sullivan's deliveryman, Sam, should return this par-ticular order to the warehouse when he'd phoned in ex-plaining that the manager of the Keys had no cash available for payment at that time. But then, how had she been supposed to know the place was presumably located in a basement.

'Ah, I forgot! You want payment in advance!' Her face must have mirrored her quandary as her visitor reached into the inside pocket of his jacket to produce a slim pack of banknotes, offering them to her with an impatient movement of his hand.

Ginny took them, withdrawing her hand quickly as inadvertently it touched his, with the startling effect of static electricity earthing. Masking her unexpected dis-comfort at the effect of the warm masculine skin against her own, she looked down at a handful of brand-new twenty-pound notes. More than enough for his present demands.

'Now—my order!'

The impatient tone commanded action.

'Very well, in the circumstances, I'll see what I can do.' Facing up to the inevitable, she shot him a quelling glance, lifting the warehouse keys from their hook, before walking sedately across the yard, uncomfortably aware of the controlled energy in every step of her irate customer as he paced beside her.

Beneath his intolerant gaze it wasn't surprising that she fumbled with the first key, only to find it didn't fit.

'Here!' Without waiting for her permission he lifted the whole bunch from her nerveless fingers, silently glancing from the padlock back to the assortment on the ring, before selecting one and pressing it into the lock, which opened instantly.

'Where do you keep them?'

'They'll still be loaded on a pallet awaiting future delivery after payment.' Irritated by his testy expulsion of breath, she added tartly, 'None of this need have happened if you'd met our terms in the first place.'

'Your *new* terms,' he stressed tightly. 'Terms of which I, as proprietor of the Keys, was totally unaware since I only returned from Athens a couple of hours ago.' He cast her a scathing look. 'What's my old friend Leo trying to do, eh? Bankrupt himself by offering less favourable contracts than his competitors? And without prior notice too?'

His denigrating words stung as she stared back into eyes, which were studying her with such patronising scrutiny that she could feel a warm flush of mortification fire her veins.

'It was *my* decision,' she confessed, springing to the rescue of her father's business integrity, wondering just how genuine the professed friendship between the two men was—if it existed at all. 'My father has granted me full autonomy to run the business in his absence——' only to have the impulsive defence of her position interrupted.

'Absence?' Dark brows met in a frown as Ginny experienced a stab of regret at allowing herself to be goaded into indiscretion.

Four days had passed since Leo Sullivan had collapsed with a perforated ulcer and he was still recovering from emergency surgery in hospital, but she hadn't meant to discuss her father's illness with anyone outside the company. It was a mistake to betray one's weaknesses— because that was when the predators moved in...

'So Leo's handed over his business to his beloved daughter, has he?' Her male antagonist looked at her broodingly. 'I hope, for his sake, it's on a purely temporary basis while he's employed gainfully elsewhere— or his indulgence looks like costing him dear.'

'That's hardly your concern.' Ginny flinched from the cool derision of the comment, smarting under his obvious contempt for her business methods, crossly aware that it might be merited.

'Right! *My* concern is to keep the Keys of Corfu open!' His beautifully moulded mouth tugged down at the corners. 'Look, lady, I've paid my cash as demanded. I want my goods—and now!' The words were ground out from between beautiful white teeth as he glowered at her flushed face.

'All right!' Although his assertion was unassailable she resented his attitude enormously, not the least because there was some justification for it, she admitted reluctantly to herself. 'It's over here.'

She only realised how closely he'd dogged her footsteps when, finding and removing the top carton, she dislodged a fat black spider. The scream that left her mouth was echoing round the warehouse before she'd even had time to think, let alone suppress it. All her life she'd been terrified of spiders. Here in this confined space her phobia was overwhelming.

Totally panic-stricken, she turned to run, only to find herself caught against a hard, warm male chest, her shoulders grasped by a pair of firm hands.

'Stay where you are—it's gone,' she was instructed calmly. 'Deafened, if not scared to death.'

'I can't stand them,' she explained needlessly, unable to hide the shudders of revulsion which still trembled through her nervous system.

'You really are terrified . . .' Her unexpected customer seemed to have forgotten his blistering hurry as his hands kept their restraining hold on her shoulders. 'I think you'd better wait in the yard while I help myself.' He eyed the stack thoughtfully. 'I'll take the table-light posies now. The balance of the order can be delivered tomorrow.'

At least her discomfiture seemed to have had the positive effect of lessening his former aggression. Knowing it was the bulk rather than the weight which made handling the large cartons difficult, Ginny regarded him doubtfully, prepared to pay a small penance for the undoubted inconvenience she had caused him.

'I'll help you load them,' she offered stiffly.

'No way!' White teeth showed in a brief, unexpected smile. 'Another spider and another scream like that, and your neighbours will think you're being attacked. You've already disrupted my life enough for one day. I've no wish to be arrested for assault.'

There was nothing improper in the gleam that illuminated his mocking eyes, but his whole manner was too blatantly masculine and aggressive for Ginny to be at ease in his presence—certainly not at such close quarters.

'I'll get your receipt, then.' She shot a haughty glance at his hands, which still rested on her arms, breathing a sigh of relief as he let her go and she was able to squeeze past him in the narrow aisle without brushing against him.

She was still writing out the receipt when he strolled back into the office. So he had the muscles of Tarzan lurking beneath his designer jacket, she determined sourly, signing her initials with a flourish. Turning to give it to him, she found to her horror that he was perched on the desk behind her, reading the list of Sullivan's outstanding debtors which Duncan produced weekly.

'Please!' She flushed scarlet at his impertinence, torn between outrage at his interference and the knowledge that she couldn't afford to offend him for a second time lest she lose his business entirely. 'That's confidential.'

'Do you know exactly how much is outstanding here?' Ignoring her protest, he waved the stapled sheets in her face as if she were some innumerate idiot.

Catching her tongue between her teeth, Ginny forced herself to remain silent, determined not to discuss the company's financial position with a stranger—and a singularly annoying one at that! If she thought she'd have any chance of success she'd try to wrest the damning evidence from his hands.

A quick look at her set face and he'd apparently formed his own opinion of her silence, continuing conversationally, 'Yes, of course you do. That's why you made the draconian and potentially lethal reforms to your credit terms.'

'If everyone paid on time they wouldn't have been necessary,' she flared.

'Exactly.' Dark eyes appraised her coolly. 'It was the defectors you should have hunted, the slow payers and the large companies whose policy it is to pay late on principle—not the small restaurants who meet their commitments as per their contracts—and certainly not without advance notice.'

'Thank you for your advice,' she said stiffly, one foot tapping impatiently as he made no move to leave. 'Didn't you say you were in a hurry?'

'I see you have a good memory,' he approved, pocketing the receipt and change without checking either. 'A big asset in business. Perhaps there's hope for you yet! Come up to London with me, and we'll discuss it over dinner.'

'What?' Astounded, she watched him replace the list of creditors before striding from the office as if her agreement were a foregone conclusion. Outside at the entrance to the yard a black Lotus Carlton crouched in powerful anticipation. Pausing, his fingers on the door-handle, he turned to face her.

Temporarily bereft of words, Ginny stared at him, part of her very angry at his outrageous behaviour, the other part wanting to laugh. Hysteria, she decided detachedly as she fought down the bubble of mirth in her diaphragm. Did he really think he was so irresistible?

Apparently so, because he made no effort to move, continuing to regard her with one eyebrow raised quizzically. 'Well?'

'Thank you, no. I've already made plans for tonight.' Conscious of the small irregular pulse fluttering at her throat, she made a show of looking at her watch. It was the truth. She'd decided to spend the rest of the evening trying to find a solution to the other calamities which

had befallen Sullivan's in her absence at university.
Calamities which her father and his small supportive staff
had colluded to keep her in ignorance about until now.

Only the delivery of an enforcement order from the
local council two days after her father had been rushed
to hospital, directing the company to clear out their
warehouses and find alternative storage facilities within
twenty-eight days, had broken that conspiracy of silence.
Until then she'd had no idea her father had been fighting
a lawsuit, or that their stock was abnormally low because a lorry containing replacements was held up in a
blockade in Europe, or the other minor but irritating
events which had plagued the business.

Irritation sharpened her tone as she reinforced her decision as politely as she could. 'And frankly I'm waiting
to lock up.'

His gaze travelled carefully from the top of her head
to her toes and back again. 'I can spare you ten minutes
to get ready,' he announced as if she'd never spoken.
Critical eyes finished their impertinent inspection as she
sucked in her breath in exasperation, before he added
inconsequentially, 'You've got a spider's web in your
hair.'

'Oh!' All other thoughts abandoned, she choked back
a scream, her hand flying to the portion of her head
where his solemn gaze rested.

'That's better.' As her anxious fingers combed through
her thick, toffee-coloured curls, their golden highlights
gleaming in the late afternoon sunshine, he offered con-
solingly, 'Probably only a dust web after all.'

'Will you please go?' Weary and stressed, her only
thought to lock up the office and walk the few yards to
the peace and security of her father's pleasant detached

house, she reiterated her decision. 'I've no intention of going anywhere with you.'

'Not even to discuss business?' Classically straight eyebrows winged upwards. 'From what I've seen I'd say you could use some! I'd like to see a full set of brochures and price lists of everything available. I'm considering expanding my business interests and I need to update my files on prospective suppliers.' The look he turned on her was bland, but he'd chosen his words carefully to insinuate that Sullivan's might lose his custom in the future if she didn't co-operate.

Deliberately she counted up to ten in an effort to control her temper. 'I see,' she said evenly when she'd successfully completed her exercise in self-discipline, allowing herself the luxury of subjecting him to the kind of insolent scrutiny he'd previously bestowed on her. Her grey eyes travelled slowly down his six feet plus, starting from his indisputably handsome face, past the elegant jacket and immaculate trousers, before returning to challenge the dark invitation behind the thick fan of eyelashes. 'And how do I know that you're who you claim to be? I don't even know your name.'

'My family name is Anastasi—my given name Steel.' He shrugged his expensively tailored shoulders. 'If your customer records file has been correctly maintained you'll find my name on it—and not only as proprietor of the Keys of Corfu, but several other restaurants throughout the country.'

Anastasi? The name was strangely familiar to her, but for the moment the context eluded her. Obviously she must have seen it on the files as he'd suggested.

'Well?' he demanded impatiently as she wavered. 'Do you want to discuss further business or not?'

On a personal level it was the last thing she wanted, but on a commercial basis what option did she have?

'I suppose I could defer my existing plans,' she offered a trifle ungraciously, anxious not to appear too accommodating. Grasping at straws was one thing, but she wasn't too confident that this particular one would be worth reaching out towards. Her annoying visitor seemed more intent on making a nuisance of himself than anything else.

'Good!' His smile was bland. 'Then may I suggest you wash your face and get your brochures without further argument, Miss Sullivan? Because if we don't get back to London before the Keys is due to open, my future business prospects may be less bright than I anticipate.'

Refusing to respond to what she supposed was intended as a pun, Ginny contented herself with giving him a stiff nod before securing the office building and warehouses. Crossing the yard, she entered her father's house via the back garden gate. It took only a brief time to phone the Keys of Corfu and confirm for a distraught-sounding manager that the patron, Mr Anastasi, had indeed driven over personally in his Lotus Carlton to pick up their vital order.

Satisfied that she'd taken sensible precautions to ensure her own safety, she made for the bathroom. Grimacing at her face in the mirror, she admitted that it did need a wash and that her customer's patronising command was not without justification. Having had a fight replacing the carbon ribbon in the electric typewriter, after Cathy, her father's secretary, had left early to pick up her grandchild from school, she'd managed to leave a couple of smutty fingerprints on her cheeks. Little wonder his ill temper had been allied to amusement!

Well—he wouldn't laugh at her appearance again! Having stripped, taken a ten-second shower and changed her undies, deftly she applied make-up, enhancing her grey eyes with gentle shadow and liberally applying mascara so that her naturally long lashes made a strong frame for them. Fortunately her hair was easy. A swift hard brush and a shake of her head and the curls fell into a becoming disorder round her regularly featured face.

It wasn't a date and she certainly wasn't dressing up for it. In fact she had no intention of having dinner at the Keys, if she could possibly avoid doing so. Because she'd spent several hours of the morning sitting at her father's bedside and the rest of the day in the office trying to come to terms with an unfamiliar system, there were several household duties screaming out for her attention. She'd make her sales pitch, she determined, and then produce an excuse and escape.

Casting a critical eye over the contents of her wardrobe, she decided she wanted something cool and practical. A navy cotton drill pencil skirt, short enough to be fashionable without revealing too much leg, teamed with a loose sleeveless navy and white striped top would do fine, she decided, anchoring the two together with a smart navy belt.

Since she'd have to make the return journey to the suburbs by rail in the cool of the evening, she grabbed the skirt's matching navy jacket, slamming her nyloned feet into low-heeled navy courts before running downstairs to collect a folder of brochures. Gathering up her shoulder-bag, she left the house, pausing only when she reached the end of the garden to take a couple of deep breaths to compose herself.

Steel Anastasi was still there, leaning against his car as, assuming an air of insouciance, she walked briskly towards him. Expecting him to glance at his watch on her reappearance, she was surprised when he merely indicated that she should enter the vehicle.

'I was as quick as I could be!' To her chagrin, the retort she'd rehearsed to combat his unforthcoming criticism slipped off her tongue before she could prevent it.

'Amazingly so.' Onyx eyes surveyed her as if she'd invited their inspection and comment as she climbed into the passenger seat. 'But even if it had taken you twice as long, any man worthy of the name would have forgiven you for the effort you've made on his behalf.' Smoothly he engaged the engine and steered the car into the road as Ginny's eyes widened in disbelief at his silky response.

'I can assure you, Mr Anastasi...' she began heatedly, seeing too late the deepening dimple at the side of his mouth, which told her his provocative comment had been deliberately intended to annoy her.

'Steel,' he said simply as she paused, the colour flushing her cheeks as she realised how readily she'd risen to his bait. 'Since this may be the beginning of a long and fruitful association, I prefer you to use my given name.'

CHAPTER TWO

'STEEL?' Ginny queried, deciding to disregard his final comment. If anyone was going to have a long and fruitful association with this man it would be her father when he was well enough to return to work, not she. Disbelief sharpened her voice as he turned the Lotus skillfully into the main road traffic. 'What kind of name is that?'

'An abbreviation of the original Greek. I find my British friends have difficulty in winding their Anglo-Saxon tongues around Stylianus. You have problems with it?'

'Not particularly.' Her eyes sought the speedometer as the car gathered speed. If the name had been of British origin she would have found its association with a tough metal pretentious, but she could hardly voice a sarcastic retort when it had resulted from her own countrymen's inability to cope with the Greek original, could she?

If her companion sensed her reservations he ignored them. 'And you, of course, are Ginette.'

Shifting her position slightly beneath the restriction of the seatbelt, which pressed uncomfortably against her curves, Ginny masked her surprise. It seemed there was some justification in his claim to be a friend of her father's after all.

'I prefer to be called Ginny,' she offered repressively, tempted to ask if he had any problems with *that*, suppressing a smile at the knowledge that if the pronunciation of Ginette had been anything to go by he did. The

Greek alphabet obviously didn't include a soft-sounding G.

'Ginny.' He repeated the diminutive, with a small nod of his head as if allocating it to memory, voicing the first consonant as if it were the 'sh' in the word 'shiver', and invoking an answering tremor to traverse her spine. How seductive he made her name sound, almost exotic, or was it the husky timbre of his voice which gave that illusion?

'So, Ginny,' he continued blithely, 'what turn in the tide of fortune has persuaded Leo Sullivan to abandon the helm of his ship?'

'To someone so incapable of steering it, you mean?' she challenged bitterly.

'That wasn't my question.'

The calmness of his reply did nothing to assuage the sense of indignation she felt. It had been what he meant, and they both knew it. She stared sightlessly out of the front windscreen. Four days since her father had asked her to cope in his absence and already, because of her inexperience caused by her long absences from home, it seemed she was guiding the company into even choppier waters.

'Well?' Steel cast her a quick glance, prompting an answer.

He was the last person she wanted as a confidant, but what option did she have? If he was the friend he claimed to be, and the little evidence she had seemed to point to that conclusion, he had the right to be told about her father's illness. Her mind skittered to embrace her problems. If only Howard had stayed in Taychapel to lend her a little moral support, she thought wearily, the odds were she wouldn't even be in the unenviable position of being dragged unwillingly up to London! But, of course, she was being selfish. The leafy lanes of Surrey had their own beauty, but were hardly comparable to that of the eternal city. She could hardly blame her fiancé for continuing with the holiday they'd planned to take together in Rome—even if she hadn't been able to go with him.

Aware of a pucker of annoyance between the dark eyes of her companion as he stared ahead, awaiting her response, she sighed: a small exhalation of surrender. 'Dad's in hospital. He collapsed with a perforated ulcer.'

'What? When did this happen? Is his condition serious?'

As they pulled up at traffic lights Steel turned to face her, concern etching lines on his forehead and tightening his sensuous mouth to a hard line.

Warming momentarily to these signs of genuine distress, Ginny forced her lips into the physical form of a small smile, despite the continuing ache in her heart. 'Four days ago. I'd been at home just over a week when he was taken ill after breakfast. He was rushed to hospital and operated on within the hour. The specialist says he's out of danger, but he's still a very sick man, needing plenty of rest, and complete freedom from worry.'

'Not an easy task for a student librarian to take on, then,' Steel observed thoughtfully, moving forward with the stream of traffic as the lights changed. 'From what I've seen the company's in a pretty bad way.'

'Graduate!' she corrected him swiftly, surprised by the evidence that not only had he known of her existence but also that she'd been reading librarianship. Presumably her father had discussed her at some length with this arrogant stranger, but then the tie between them was so strong that Leo Sullivan needed little encouragement to extol the virtues—real or imagined—of his only daughter! 'What you saw was confidential!' she continued crisply, anger at his cruel percipience bringing a quick flush of colour to her cheeks. Thank heavens that, in a fit of desperation, she'd already torn down the enforcement notices which the council's agents had tacked on to the warehouse doors. A futile act, she'd recognised immediately, but one that had given her an instant if not lasting gratification.

At least her condescending companion could have no idea just how bad the situation was. Swiftly she dragged her thoughts back to the present.

'I'm confident I can cope,' she said briskly. 'Provided there aren't any rumours put about that the company's cash flow is in trouble. That would only make matters worse.'

'So will demanding money with menaces!' His gaze raked over her briefly. 'Good God, Ginny. If you insist on holding your regular customers to ransom you'll destroy the goodwill Leo's built up over the years. It's a pity you didn't learn how to deal with account books rather than how to catalogue fiction!'

The dark features were taut and unrelenting in their condemnation, and she turned her head wearily away from them, choosing to watch the monotonous stream of traffic. His judgement was simplistic and deliberately phrased to be insulting, but basically he was right. She should have stayed in Taychapel and learned the business instead of going to university. That way she could have repaid some of the devotion which her father had given her in a tangible and constructive way. Unfortunately her father had thought otherwise. Unable to go into higher education himself, he had been delighted when her skills at English literature and research had resulted in her being offered a place at a Midlands university and he'd insisted that she accept it.

Now here she was at the age of twenty-two with a degree but with no sound commercial experience to aid her in finding a way out of Sullivan's present difficulties. Not that she intended admitting to Neanderthal man sitting beside her that she agreed with him. Not after his scathing and totally unjustified criticism of her hard-won qualifications!

The rest of the journey progressed in silence until the car came to a smooth halt in the private car park of a restaurant in the heart of London's theatreland, to be greeted by a middle-aged mustachioed man who emerged from the portals, agitation clearly mirrored on his dark face.

'Kyrie Anastasi—*doksa to Theo!*'

'Relax, Kostas! Not only have I brought you your table decorations, but also the young lady who refused to let you have them, so you may tell her to her face what you think of her action.'

Ginny heaved a sigh. Was there to be no let-up in the condemnation showered upon her?

'Kyrie Anastasi...' The man seemed embarrassed.

'Still——' Steel opened the door of the passenger seat, taking Ginny's arm supportively as she alighted '—since her beauty outweighs her ignorance, we will forgive her this time, *ne?*' His tone became brisker. 'Now while you get everything unloaded and set up, Miss Sullivan and I have business to do.'

It was darker inside than she'd expected and for the first time she realised just how important the table decorations with their integral lamps were to supplement the existing wall-lights. Little wonder Steel had been so abrasive, she allowed reluctantly. Neither was she looking forward to the rest of the evening. She had a nasty suspicion that his intention was to humble her further with her lack of knowledge. As for that crack about her beauty! That had been sarcastic and completely uncalled for! She was the archetypal 'girl next door', medium height, medium colouring and, as far as Steel Anastasi was concerned, less than medium intelligence!

Half an hour later, seated in a small office behind the main restaurant, she felt even less kindly towards her abductor. For over an hour he'd looked at brochures, checked price lists and asked her interminable, relentless questions about anything and everything to do with the business, a great number of which she'd been unable to answer satisfactorily. If he'd intended to demolish her self-confidence he was certainly doing a hatchet job.

Be positive, she instructed herself silently, calling on hitherto unrealised depths of determination, as he asked yet another question to which she had no ready reply.

'Look...' She spoke forcefully, leaning forward in her eagerness, her face flushed, her eyes sparkling from the challenge of trying to salvage a sales opportunity which she sensed was rapidly slipping away from her. 'If you know Dad so well, then you also know that Duncan, our bookkeeper, has been with him for fifteen years and knows the company as well as anyone. I've noted all your questions and I can guarantee to come back to you tomorrow morning with all the information you need.'

'But until your father comes out of hospital *you* still intend to take over his role?' His tone was harsh, sceptical—inciting her to combat.

'Yes!' She glared at the patronising amusement she detected in his dark eyes. So she wasn't word perfect! After all, she was playing the part without rehearsal. A circumstance she had every intention of changing at the earliest possible moment, particularly since her father was now out of danger and she would have more time to devote to work.

'Then you've got a lot of homework to do,' came the succinct retort, as if he'd guessed her thoughts.

'I'm aware of that,' she flung back heatedly, in no mood to be lectured by this elegantly clad, arrogant Greek with his lazy smile and softly evaluating eyes. 'And since it's obvious that you don't have the slightest intention of placing an order with me, I mean to go home right now and do just that.'

Rising to her feet, she swept the spare brochures together, thrusting them back into their folder, her fingers shaking with suppressed anger and tiredness.

'No—I think not.' He was on his feet, moving with a swift grace to stand blocking her exit, hands thrust into his hip pockets, his thoughtful glance resting on her angry face. 'I invited you to have dinner with me and you accepted,' he reminded her softly.

'Only so we could discuss business—which we've now done.'

'On the contrary. I only agreed to discuss business on the understanding that you dined with me,' he returned equably.

'Then I'm sorry to disappoint you.' Damn him! He couldn't enforce her unwilling presence any longer. 'As far as I'm concerned, it was business that brought me here. I've told you what's available, so now I'm leaving.'

'Meaning that you're not?' The soft question was so unexpected that momentarily she was too confused to answer it. 'Come, Ginny. It's dinner I'm offering you— not bed and breakfast. You wouldn't want to alienate a valuable customer, would you?'

The question was gently posed, but the threat was there—not only apparent in the razor edge of his voice but also in the power of his narrowed gaze.

'You wouldn't cancel your orders with us for such a trivial reason...' Ginny stared at him aghast. 'Not after claiming to be Dad's friend?'

'I repeat that claim. On a personal level I find Leo a highly compatible companion, but haven't you heard the saying that there's no compassion in business?'

'Or integrity either by the sound of it!' she stormed back, glad to see from the expression on his face that her comment had made its mark.

None knew better than she that there were other suppliers entering the market ready and keen to take their business. It was only the efficiency of Sullivan's and the personal respect in which Leo Sullivan was held by his customers which had kept them viable in changing trading conditions. Plus, of course, the superior quality of the products they imported from the Far East, and for which they were sole agents in the UK.

Suddenly she was unsure, furious with herself because she didn't know the full extent of Steel Anastasi's influence. Hadn't he said several other restaurants throughout the country? How many might he have? Neither had his snide reference to bed and breakfast escaped her notice. Was she supposed to be grateful that he wasn't demanding sexual favours in exchange for the prospect of future business?

'I'm not bluffing, Ginny.' He'd read her fear and intensified it with such casual softness that a shiver traversed her spine. 'When you get to know me better, you'll know that's not how I operate.'

'I don't want to know you better—I'm not impressed by blackmail!' She was shaking inwardly but damned if she would meekly give in to his arrogant demands.

Black eyebrows rose in assumed amazement. 'Blackmail? What a churlish description of a simple transference of favours—your company at my table in exchange for an increased order book for Sullivan's.'

It was then she realised that he was paying her back in her own coin, using her own methods, which he had deplored, driving his point home in a way she would remember.

'That's right, Ginny.' His face was grave but his eyes mocked her with their laughter. 'Payment before delivery. A simple enough concept, but one which can be both annoying and inconvenient, when one has made other plans. However, in this instance I already have your agreement, no? Or when you spoke about lack of integrity in business were you referring to your own behaviour?'

He was proving what she already suspected. Steel Anastasi would not be a good loser and there was too much at stake for her to gamble. He'd left her no choice, she mused, furious at the way he was using her own tactics against her.

'All right.' She surrendered her position with as much dignity as she could muster. 'Since it obviously means so much to you, then I accept your invitation.'

'Good! Then shall we take our table?'

Head held high, she tired to banish the memory of the quick flash of triumph which had illuminated his face at her capitulation as she allowed herself to be led into the restaurant, impressed against her will by the difference the table lamps and floral decorations had made not only to the available light, but to the whole ambience, softening corners, lending intimacy without glare, subtly introducing the feel of the Eastern Mediterranean into the heart of metropolitan London.

Already tables were occupied, the hum of conversation spiced with guttural Greek consonants as they reached a corner table. It wasn't just a tourist place, then, but a favorite of the local Greek community as well, she decided, seating herself on a comfortably upholstered bench seat, noting as she did so the high quality of the table linen, the gleaming cutlery and the sparkling crystal of the glasses.

Steel followed her gaze as she absorbed the atmosphere. 'It's been closed for a week for improvements to the kitchen and redecoration,' he explained, adding drily, 'It will look better still when I receive the rest of my order from Sullivan's.' He pointed to where an unadorned trellis lay skeletal against a white archway leading to the bar, and bare alcoves beyond it stood stark against softly cushioned chairs. 'Living plants would be preferable but, without daylight, impossible, so it's a case of allowing art to mirror art—only in this case, as you are aware, the *art* I required was delayed at source!' He smiled, giving her the full benefit of his excellent teeth. 'Do you wish to see the menu or would you prefer to select directly from the kitchen?'

She shrugged. 'I'm not really hungry. Moussaka will do fine—I suppose you do serve that?'

'Of course.' Steel's dark head inclined politely, but the glint in his eyes and the slight tightening of his jaw suggested her studied indifference irritated him, as did his barbed reply. 'It's the only Greek dish most English people have heard of.'

'Hardly surprising. Greek cuisine isn't famed for its variety or excellence, is it?' she retorted sweetly, beginning to enjoy this verbal sparring. 'Moussaka is a kind of shepherd's pie, isn't it? Well, since that's what I was going to have for dinner tonight anyway, I might just as well have it here.'

'Let's hope you won't be disappointed. What would you like with it—chips?'

A gleam of overt contempt in his coal-dark eyes branded her a philistine, tempting her to accept his suggestion for the pure pleasure of annoying him further. She could even ask for some tomato ketchup, she considered wickedly. On the other hand, she was beginning to find his narrow-eyed stare discouraging. It could be a mistake to bait him too openly.

'I'd prefer a salad—if I may?' she returned meekly, flashing him an insincere smile.

'Of course.' There was a cool edge of irony in his reply. 'You'll excuse me if I leave you for a few moments to make my own choice.'

It wasn't a question and Ginny didn't reply, watching him as he eased his athletic body between the tables and chairs to make his leisurely way towards the kitchen.

In other circumstances she would have enjoyed dining at the Keys, she allowed reluctantly. But her plans had been so disrupted during the last few days that she felt disorientated, unable to exercise her usual control over her life. Idly she moved the silk posy, her eyes dwelling on the soft battery-operated lamp which illuminated its fragile beauty.

What was Howard doing now, she wondered, alone in Rome? She'd half expected he'd telephone her on arrival two days ago, but there'd been no call. Her lips twisted ruefully as she conjured up a picture of him in her mind's eye. Howard always seemed such a tower of strength. Strong in both mind and body. A positive person, well-established in his career as sports master at an exclusive private school, a formidable oarsman and tennis player, as well as having a long list of academic achievements. A man who controlled every aspect of his life with the efficiency of a good accountant...

So why was she finding it necessary to itemise all his good points? Her gaze lingered on the light. And why, despite her understanding of his attitude, did she still feel so hurt? Of course the old concept that women should turn to men for comfort and support when trouble struck no longer applied, and she had no argument in principle with that. It was just that if their positions had been reversed—if someone close to Howard had become desperately ill—she wouldn't have thought twice about giving up her holiday to stay with him and do what she could to help and support him, practically as well as emotionally.

But then their relationship had never been particularly physical. Moving uneasily, unable to relax, she wondered miserably, not for the first time, if Howard's self-control sprang from the fact that he found her more socially acceptable than physically irresistible!

Until now she'd supposed his apparent respect for her lack of sexual experience was based on consideration for the ideals instilled in her in childhood, an instinctive awareness that her innate passion would bloom more readily and luxuriantly within the framework of marriage.

As a teenager she'd been shy and apprehensive in the company of men. Not for her the casual relationships or intense physical intimacy her girlfriends had embraced with such enthusiasm. In retrospect, she realised that if her mother hadn't died when she'd been so young she might have been more at ease with her own budding sexuality than the prosaic hygiene lessons at school allied to her father's euphemistic generalities had encouraged her to be.

As it was, she'd flinched from physical contact with the adolescent youths who'd attempted to court her with a callow lack of sophistication, and found escape in reading and studying...

How ironic it was, then, that she'd finally decided to abandon the principles which the majority of her contemporaries found quaint and unsustainable, only to discover that Howard preferred a lonely bed in Rome to becoming her lover in Taychapel!

'Kyrie Anastasi has ordered this wine for you—shall I pour it now?'

Immersed in her thoughts, Ginny hadn't seen the waiter approach.

Nodding her assent, she watched as her glass was filled from the newly opened bottle. Doubtless Steel had already tasted and approved it, she thought sourly.

'The patron sends his apologies. Unfortunately he has been delayed, but will be with you as soon as possible.'

Dipping her head in silent acknowledgement, Ginny took a sip of the wine. It was cool, dry and wonderfully refreshing.

Involved in attempting to analyse her feelings for Howard, she hadn't realised how long she'd been left alone. Still, the longer she was deprived of Steel Anastasi's company the better! He might be able to command her presence, but he couldn't command her pleasure, and when he did deign to reappear she'd continue to make that quite clear to him.

She took another sip of wine, following it with a much longer one, her body relaxing at last as it teased her palate, awakening her taste-buds.

'I see you approve of my choice, then?'

She jumped as the silky question was whispered close to her ear. Staring too long at the small light, she hadn't observed Steel's return. So much for her intended pretence that she wasn't impressed by his selection.

'It's quite pleasant,' she told him repressively, deciding to damn with faint praise.

'There was a crisis in the kitchen,' he offered as explanation, seating himself opposite her. 'One of the girls had befriended a stray kitten. When she discovered I was on the premises, she panicked and hid it in a cupboard. Unfortunately, it took exception to being imprisoned and created havoc.' The stern tone warned her that dire consequences had ensued as he filled and lifted his own glass.

As she stared in horror at his long, taut fingers as they caressed the crystal stem, a wave of faintness made Ginny clutch her own glass more tightly. Heaven forbid he'd wrung the poor little creature's neck before returning to the table!

'What did you do?' It was as much as she could do to whisper the question.

'What do you suppose?' His deep-set eyes taunted her for the sentiment which drew lines of concern across her forehead. 'Dispensed with the services of both of them, of course. The girl and the cat.'

CHAPTER THREE

'YOU dismissed her?'

'She disobeyed me!' His face was expressionless, unresponsive to Ginny's implied criticism.

'That's the ultimate crime, is it?' she enquired icily, unable to restrain her immediate reaction to the clipped authority of Steel's tone.

'Yes. Particularly when as a result of it the local authorities could close the Keys down for hygiene infringements.'

The flat finality in the timbre of his voice forbade her to question his judgement. His logic was harsh but, she supposed grudgingly, basically sound. It still seemed a cruel punishment for an impulsive act of kindness.

'Will you give the girl a reference so she can apply for work elsewhere?' she enquired tartly, convinced she already knew the answer.

'No.' He shook his head, confirming the impression she'd already formed about his lack of charity.

'But surely——' she began heatedly, determined not to be quelled by his black expression.

A slight movement of his free hand pre-empted the objection which rose to her lips. 'Unnecessary, because after due consideration I re-employed her.'

'Compassion, Steel?' Allowing her amazement to show, Ginny permitted her gaze to linger on the powerful cast of his face. 'I'd imagined you incapable of such a human feeling.'

34

'And you were right, Ginny.' His answering smile had an edge as sharp as a razor. 'She was re-employed because she's good at her job, and it would be a waste of time and resources to train another person to her standard. Besides, since she's now in my debt her future behaviour will be exemplary.'

'And the kitten?' Ginny pursued doggedly.

'You expect me to put that on the payroll?' He mocked her concern with open amusement. 'Or are you afraid it will become an ingredient in your moussaka?'

'Neither.' She rose to his challenge, making no attempt to hide her disapproval of his flippancy. 'Since either solution would put you out of business! What I would *hope* is that, having evicted it, you'd do your best to find a good home for it.'

'If the promise of such an action will remove the scowl from your pretty face, then I make it to you.' The even whiteness of his unexpected smile disarmed her completely, forcing her to make a concerted effort to regain her composure as he continued easily, 'Now we've disposed of business matters and appeased your sentimental conscience, we will enjoy our meal and get to know each other better.'

It was fortunate, Ginny thought grimly, that the waiter arrived at their table at that precise moment bearing a tray laden with dishes of Greek starters. At least she could comply with one of Steel Anastasi's requirements, she accorded philosophically; the food looked delicious. As for getting to know him better—she'd prefer to be on intimate terms with a boa constrictor!

To her surprise he made no further move to engage her in conversation until they'd both finished their main course.

'How fortunate for your father that you were actually at home when he became ill,' he remarked casually, placing his knife and fork tidily on his plate. 'It must be a great comfort to him that, in his hour of need, Sullivan's is being supervised by his own flesh and blood.'

The irony of the statement wasn't lost on her, her ego shrivelling beneath his patronising gaze. So, she'd made an error in judgement, she allowed reluctantly. It didn't mean she was entirely worthless!

'Yes, it is,' she agreed steadily. 'And what's more I intend to prove myself deserving of his trust.' Unable to suppress the sudden shudder which convulsed her as she relived the horror of her father's unexpected collapse, she added on a rising note of anguish, 'Another few days and Howard and I would have been in Rome, enjoying ourselves, totally unaware that——'

'Howard?' Steel swooped on the name, his dark gaze clashing enquiringly with her own troubled eyes. 'Who is Howard?'

'He—I . . .' she began, aware that she owed this patronising Greek nothing, least of all a detailed account of her personal affairs. How could she discuss Howard or his role in her life with Steel Anastasi? Quite apart from the fact that it would be extremely disloyal of her, she must remember that beneath her host's elegant clothes there dwelt the soul of the angry dictator who'd stormed down to the suburbs intent on getting his own way, the ruthless barbarian who'd flung a helpless kitten out into the night.

If she needed a confidant—and a small inner voice prompted her that she might—then this autocratic Greek was the last person to fill the role! On the other hand— her thoughts took off at a tangent—perhaps the introduction of a fiancé might serve to emphasise the fact that she was not without male support should her masterful escort have thought otherwise!

In the end it was the proprietorial gleam in Steel's discerning eyes which decided the issue. 'Howard is the man I intend to marry,' she informed him coolly.

Black eyebrows flared incredulously. 'You don't wear his ring.'

Trust his sharp eyes to notice that! 'It's not obligatory.' She dismissed the observation with a wave of the hand on which he'd fastened his gaze. She was certainly not going to tell him that their engagement hadn't ever been officially announced, but was more an understanding between them—an assumption made by their friends and subliminally accepted by both of them.

'If you were my betrothed, Ginny, you'd most certainly wear my ring.' As the corners of Steel's shapely mouth curled upwards, so something deep inside Ginny seemed to curl in unison, or perhaps it was the husky, intimate sound of her name on his tongue which affected her.

'Well, I'm not!' she snapped, horrified to discover that, incredible though it was, she was finding Steel Anastasi physically attractive! But there was no need to be upset by a purely endocrine reaction, was there? But she *was* upset, because Howard was gorgeous, like a Nordic god, but never once had she experienced this strange melting of her insides when he smiled at her.

'So where is this Howard now?' Steel's expression held a note of mockery. 'Don't tell me he went to Rome without you?'

'Of course, why not?' Ginny tried to invoke some enthusiasm into her voice, but even to her own ears it sounded forced. 'Howard's a teacher, not a businessman. There was nothing he could do here.'

Desperately she stared at the empty plate that had supported her moussaka—as far removed from shepherd's pie as she could imagine—with its spicy meat, succulent aubergines and thick, creamy cheese topping. Perhaps it was the herbs in it that had awakened this strange reaction she was experiencing towards the domineering Greek seated opposite her...

'Do you want some more?'

'What?' Startled from her reverie, she raised her eyes to meet Steel's earnest regard, unable to hide the betraying rush of colour to her face as she sought to apply his question to the path of her wayward thoughts.

'Moussaka,' he prompted gently. 'You were looking at your plate with such blatant hunger, I wondered if you wanted a second helping.'

'No—no, thank you.' Swiftly Ginny regathered her thoughts. 'Just coffee will be fine—English style if you have it.'

A snap of his fingers brought the waiter to his side at the same moment as the wall-lights dimmed and three chairs were brought on to the centre part of the restaurant floor, which had been cleared.

'You provide a floor show too?' She gave way to a sudden impulse to taunt her supercilious companion. 'Let me guess—one of the waiters dances and we all throw plates?'

'No.' The look he bestowed on her was condescending and derisive. 'That's an old Greek custom that's been vastly overdone by foreigners without a proper Greek reason.'

'There has to be a reason?'

'Most definitely.' There was a spark of some indefinable emotion in the gaze to which she was subjected.
'We call it *kefi*. A magic, ancient type of phenomenon—
difficult to translate—it descends without warning, runs
its due course and disappears. I suppose one might call
it possession by the spirit of happiness...' She was aware
of a sudden strange quality of intensity which held Steel's
body in thrall as he stared into her face, commanding
her attention. 'It can't be bought or forced and some
people never know it in a lifetime. But to be possessed
by *kefi* is to know that life is for living joyfully, is to be
a free spirit at one with the ancient gods.'

'And that allows a person to throw plates and glasses
at random?'

Denying the strange thrill which seemed to have elec-
trified every cell in her body, Ginny fought to appear
unimpressed. Unable to explain to herself why she felt
a need to prick Steel Anastasi's complacency, she sensed
subconsciously that here was an opportunity to do so
with the greatest impact.

Wide shoulders shrugged dismissively. 'Perhaps you
have to be born Greek to understand.' He leaned towards her across the table, drawing her into his own
magnetic field, compelling her attention with the sheer
force of his purpose. 'It's symbolic, accomplished within
its own internal rhythm. It can never be truly simulated
for tourist audiences.' Deep and low, his voice assaulted
her senses, commanding her attention, as if willing her
understanding.

Perhaps it was the smoky atmosphere or the soft
lighting but his face seemed very close to her, his slightly
parted lips issuing an invitation which had nothing to
do with speech. Across the small table his body was

communicating with hers with an animal magnetism which was both frightening and entrancing.

Aware that her feelings towards him were becoming more confused by the second, Ginny made a supreme effort to drag herself back to reality. Her bizarre reactions were caused by tiredness, she told herself as she fought against the strange, compelling charm of her unsolicited host.

Afraid and bewildered by the emotions he had stirred within her, she struck out wildly, intent on self-preservation.

'What's so Greek about that?' she demanded scornfully, pleased with the way she managed to master the incipient trembling of her larynx. 'We have a similar phenomenon here in England. We call it vandalism.'

There was a long, agonising silence as unhurriedly Steel studied her face feature by feature, until his cool scrutiny became too much to bear and she looked away.

'I'm sorry,' he said at last in a voice so devoid of emotion that it was as if a cold wind enveloped her, chilling her blood. Her attempt to score against him had succeeded only too well—but to her shocked surprise she found no pleasure in his reaction, only an aching emptiness in her heart as he continued quietly, 'Clearly there is nothing about my country or my culture which you find appealing—or even tolerable. Finish your coffee and I'll take you back to your own environment.'

If he'd slapped her face, the colour which rose to her cheeks could not have been more pronounced. She'd wanted to oppose him, rebel against the way he had intruded into her life, and she'd succeeded, so why did she feel so devastated by his response to her tartness?

Bewildered by the pain the backlash of his displeasure had caused her, Ginny took a sip of coffee, wincing as the hot liquid scorched her tongue.

Regret tearing bitterly at her heart, she found herself unable to bear the smouldering disdain of his cold-eyed stare, choosing instead to look beyond him towards the centre floor place where two musicians had entered, each carrying the mandolin-type bouzouki, and were seating themselves. Behind them came a woman—small, plump and dark-haired. Simply dressed in black, she took up her position behind the third chair, holding lightly on to its back rail.

There was a brief pause as the hum of conversation subsided, then the bouzoukis burst into life and the woman began to sing. Her voice was coarse yet passionate, deep but womanly as it moved dextrously through a scale of notes which owed as much to the musical style of the East as to the West. There was no need for Ginny to understand the words as the music sobbed and soared. Instinctively, she knew she was listening to the outpouring of a tragedy so intense that it was unbearable for the sufferer.

Steel, too, was watching the performer, enabling her to study his profile unobserved, appreciating the balance and symmetry of the strong features, the mask-like perfection of his carved bones and the lush softness of the hair which softened their outline.

She'd been prejudiced by his initial anger, irritated by his arrogance, but the face turned away from her at that moment was solemn and sensitive, and it was doing strange things to her ability for judgement.

When her tears came they were like a tropical storm, unexpected and tumultuous. She wept silently—because

her father was so dreadfully ill, because the business he
loved was in peril, because she was tired and because
she'd fooled herself into believing that she loved Howard
and now she was beginning to realise that whatever
emotion she felt for him it wasn't enough—would never
be enough . . .

She cried too because in some strange way she realised
the man sitting opposite her with his proud profile
averted from her gaze had acted as the final catalyst in
that realisation and she wished with all her heart that
she'd never met him!

A small sob must have escaped her because suddenly
Steel moved, sliding on to the seat beside her, placing
his firm arm round her shoulders as she scrabbled in her
bag to find a tissue. It was the final humiliation, as he
drew her close with a deadly purpose, his other hand
finding and lifting a spotless white table napkin to her
cheeks to mop at their dampness.

Applause swelled to commend the singer as the last
aching note of her song died into silence, and it was all
Ginny could do to prevent her weary body from straining
against Steel's strong frame in its urge to find solace for
her misery.

'So,' he chided her softly, his expression enigmatic,
'you are not indifferent to the pain and passion of the
ribetico. Perhaps there is hope for you after all, Ginny.'

'Perhaps there is.' She tried to smile, but when she
lifted her eyes to meet his the unexpected softness mirrored there took her by surprise, then he was drawing
her into his embrace, sighing as her unresisting body gave
up the struggle to oppose him.

In that instant she was conscious only of the comfort
he offered her, her hands finding harbour against his

upper arms as she accepted it, burying her face against his shoulder, feeling the heat from his sweet skin warming her through the fresh linen.

When his hand stroked her tumbled hair away from her cheek she took it as a signal that the time had come to leave, and opened her lips to tell him that she could make her own way home. But the words were never spoken as he covered her protest with his own mouth. Her senses spinning, Ginny knew she should protest, but as the applause died and the bouzoukis recommenced their strumming and the beat of the *ribetico* mingled in her ears with the steady hammer of Steel's heart she knew she'd left it too late to speak.

It was late when the Keys closed. How late Ginny had no way of knowing, since she'd forgotten to replace her watch on her wrist after her shower. She only knew that, encouraged by an appreciative audience, the *ribetico* singer had delivered an extensive repertoire, and that long after she'd finished her own coffee Steel had introduced her to another speciality of his country—a small measure of alcohol called *raki*, a mixture of fire and ice which had taken her breath away.

For the first time since her father's illness and the revelation about the precarious state of his business, she felt relaxed, floating free. Yet behind the feeling of lethargy there was a sense of excitement, as if something new and wonderful had entered her life for the first time. Tentatively she touched her lips with the tip of her tongue. Beside her Steel turned his head, his mouth twisting into a knowing smile that betrayed his knowledge of her thoughts, and sent a curl of sensation rippling through her nervous system.

'Time to go, sweetheart.' He rose to his feet with leisurely grace. 'I'm sure you'll agree the evening wasn't wasted after all.'

It was no time to argue the point, not when she suspected that Steel's reaction to the expression of her pent-up grief had held more than a touch of retribution about it, a hint of the conqueror enforcing his superiority on the conquered.

Taking her seat in the Lotus, she shivered. Steel Anastasi wasn't a man to be baited with impunity; his icy reaction to her flip suggestion that there was little to choose between *kefi* and vandalism had proved that without a doubt. Now she could only hope that his claim that the evening had been well spent meant that she'd been successful in retaining his custom.

She must have drifted off to sleep during the journey to the suburbs because the next thing she was aware of was that Steel had parked the car neatly outside her father's house and was calling her name gently to awaken her.

'Will you come in for a few minutes?' Still half asleep, she struggled to be polite. The least she could do was offer him a cup of coffee before he drove back to London.

An animal awareness flared suddenly in the dark eyes which surveyed her, causing a sense of imminent danger to penetrate her stupor. In that instant, fear twisted in Ginny's heart and found an echo on the white stillness of her face.

'Not tonight, Ginny.' Swiftly Steel rejected her hospitality, his expression shuttered, the threat diminished. 'The offer this time was dinner, not bed and break-fast—remember?'

Oh, how dared he misunderstand her like that? Angrily she turned from him, fully alert now, her fingers seeking and finding the front-door key in her purse, turning it quickly in the lock to regain the fastness of her own domain, his soft laugh still echoing in her embarrassed ears as she gained sanctuary and slammed the door behind her.

Having set her alarm clock for eight the following morning, she awakened seconds before it went off, dragging herself into the bathroom to regard her face with a small moan of self-contempt.

Ashamed was too weak a word to describe the way she felt. Yet her reflection told her that the first good night's sleep she'd had for a week had been beneficial to her. Gone was the drawn look that had made the hollows in her cheeks seem deeper, and her eyes sparkled with a clarity which denied her the comfort of believing that her bizarre behaviour of the previous evening had been due to having too much to drink.

Stoically she showered, dressed and made herself a piece of toast, disgusted that she could feel hungry after the spectacle she had made of herself. If crying in public weren't bad enough, the memory of that compelling, rapacious kiss Steel had given her made her squirm with embarrassment. She didn't even have the consolation of knowing she'd tried to prevent it!

On the contrary, she accused herself remorselessly, she'd done just the opposite, allowing her lips to part in welcome abandonment to Steel's practised assault. The truth was, she'd offered her mouth shamelessly to the skilled embrace of a virtual stranger, and his wholehearted acceptance of her invitation was something she wasn't going to forget in a hurry!

She gulped down a mouthful of coffee. If all that hadn't been bad enough, she'd made the fatal mistake of attempting to be courteous to him and he'd had the gall to misread her intentions and to *reject* what he had supposed to be an invitation to share her bed! In future she'd make quite sure their paths never crossed.

In future. Her bristling vexation subsided. What kind of future was there for Sullivan's unless she could raise enough money within the next twenty-eight days to lodge an appeal against the enforced closure of the warehouses?

The sound of the early morning post falling on the mat raised her spirits. Perhaps it would contain some long-overdue payments. Hastily discarding the obvious circulars, she gathered the remaining letters together, returning to the living-room to sort through them methodically. Nothing. Not one cheque among them, and the only envelope left bore a postmark which announced its point of origin as being the Far East. Orchid International, Sullivan's largest and most prestigious supplier. Surely not another bill? Her fingers tightened on the envelope as a wave of nausea surged through her body, only to fade as she remembered Duncan telling her that Sullivan's had paid for all its existing stock.

It was therefore with no real sense of foreboding that she opened the envelope and withdrew the single sheet of letter heading—only to gasp out loud in shock as she read its contents: 'Unless a guarantee of larger sales can be given and honoured in line with our contract, we will have no option but to sever our sole agency with you.'

Her mind in a turmoil, Ginny groped for a chair, lowering her shaking body into it. So it had come to this.

Even if by some miracle she could find enough money to fight the enforcement order and keep the yard and warehouses open, unless she could expand their sales base without delay, there would be no future stock to fill them!

CHAPTER FOUR

IT WAS dark by the time Ginny parked her father's Renault in the forecourt of his house that night. Relaxing for a few moments in the comfort of the driving seat, she reviewed the past day's success-rate. It could have been worse, she consoled herself. It had been an inspiration to drive up to the Midlands—a territory she'd become increasingly familiar with during her university days. She'd discovered and converted six new restaurants to Sullivan's products on a trial basis, not one of them giving her half as hard a time as the proprietor of the Keys of Corfu!

It was a start to achieving new business, and, considering she'd been calling 'cold', she supposed she should be pleased with her efforts. Tomorrow, she determined, she'd stay in the office and go through the card file of existing customers in an effort to identify those who hadn't ordered for some time and try to regain their patronage. Since Steel's cruel exposure of her previous plan as untenable, it was the only road open to her. Wearily she hauled her aching body from the car and entered the dark house.

Without Leo's presence it was cold and empty, almost menacing, and she was glad to seek the comfort of her own bedroom and the solace of a night's sleep after a day of strenuous effort.

However, by eight-thirty the next morning her usual enthusiasm and optimism had returned to sustain her.

Dressed comfortably in faded jeans and a blue and white checked cotton blouse knotted at her waist, in preparation for a day's hard work in the office, she was finishing a breakfast of toast and marmalade washed down by black coffee, when the doorbell rang.

Not more disastrous news by post! Her coffee-cup still grasped in her hand, she opened the front door only to step back in astonishment.

'So you finally made it home.' Apparently reading her retreat as an invitation to enter, Steel Anastasi stepped over the threshold. Casually dressed in grey cotton trousers and a lemon and grey T-shirt which stretched smoothly across his wide shoulders, a mile away from his earlier sartorial elegance, he still projected an image of polished confidence. 'And have you been successful in your campaign to rescue Sullivan's from bankruptcy?'

'My actions are none of your concern!' Incensed by his sardonic expression, she threw the words at him like projectiles, rising furiously to the challenge of his enquiry as she realised he must have questioned the office staff about her whereabouts the previous day. 'What are you doing here anyway? The office doesn't open until nine and I don't do business from my personal residence——'

'Not even personal business?' he interrupted smoothly. 'You left something behind at the Keys.'

'I did?' Taken by surprise, she frowned. 'What?'

'It's in the car. Come!' An imperious movement of his head demanded her compliance.

She would have liked to refuse, but at least it would be one way of getting him out of the house. Best to comply with his wishes and dismiss him politely when he returned her belongings—though heaven alone knew what she could have left—unless it was some of her brochures... With a sigh of resignation she dumped her coffee-mug on the hall table and followed him out to the forecourt, where the Lotus gleamed broodingly beside the more sedate Renault.

'I'm afraid it doesn't travel very well,' he remarked casually, the bulk of his shoulders blocking her view as he reached inside to the back seat of the luxury model.

Travel well? Intrigued despite her antipathy towards him, Ginny waited as he straightened and turned to confront her. Inside the cradle of his arms a small bundle of black fur regarded her through suspicious emerald eyes.

'I promised I'd find a good home for him,' Steel reminded her smugly. He inclined his dark head to indicate the front door ajar behind her. 'This is it.'

'The kitten from the Keys? You want me to have him?' Momentarily she floundered, as much astonished that he'd acted on his guarantee so swiftly as by the pragmatic way he'd honoured his undertaking.

Steel nodded. 'I decided it was the simplest way to convince you I'd kept my word.' The innocent explanation was accompanied by a suspicious twitch of the corners of his mouth and a glint at the back of his ebony eyes which challenged her to refuse his unsolicited gift.

Overwhelmed by a surge of compassion, Ginny determined to ignore the implicit provocation plastered on Steel's handsome face. 'Of course I'll give him a home!' she vowed. 'Does he have a name?'

'Not one in polite use, I'm afraid. How about Kefi?' he suggested drily. 'He certainly vandalised my kitchen last night. He hasn't exactly behaved himself on the drive over either. Did you know that cats could be car sick?'

'Oh, no!' Ginny glanced at the interior of the Lotus with genuine concern, deciding to ignore his barbed remark as to the origin of the kitten's proposed name. 'Your beautiful car!'

'There's no damage done—here...'

Dumping the dejected bundle in her welcoming arms, he reached inside the vehicle, emerging with a basket filled with newspaper and a couple of tins of cat food. 'At least he had the decency to stay in his basket until he felt better.' Screwing up the paper, he dumped it in the refuse bin against the garage door.

Anxious though she was to escape from his disquieting presence, Ginny realised that social etiquette demanded that she invite him back into the house, despite the deep instinct which warned her that to do so was to invite danger. A warm, enticing danger, but danger none the less.

Conscious of the nervous dryness of her mouth, she managed to keep her voice coolly impersonal, determined that this time there'd be no mistaking what was on offer. 'I expect you'd like to clean your hands. If you care to use the bathroom, I'll make you a cup of coffee before you leave.'

'Thank you.' His dark head inclined graciously as he accepted her hospitality.

Having directed him to the bathroom, Ginny carried the now struggling kitten into the kitchen, delighted to discover that it had already regained its land legs and, with small tail erect, was eager to explore its new surroundings.

A few minutes later its donor returned from the bathroom and seated himself on one of the high kitchen stools, legs stretched out, completely at ease.

'It'll have to be instant,' Ginny remarked defensively. 'I haven't got round to stocking up the larder yet—— Oh!'

As she reached behind Steel's broad back to grasp the coffee-jar, her eyes focused in horror on a dark stain which blemished the soft cotton of the T-shirt stretched over his shoulder-blade.

'You're bleeding!' she exclaimed in spontaneous dismay, placing an impulsive finger lightly on the discoloured area, withdrawing it quickly as the warmth of Steel's skin assaulted its tip.

'I told you Kefi wasn't a good passenger.' He shrugged dismissively. 'When he'd recovered from his digestive upset, he insisted on spending the rest of the journey hunched on my shoulder. Unfortunately, I had to brake suddenly and he had problems with his balancing act.'

'Oh, dear.' Laughter gurgled in Ginny's throat at the picture the succinct explanation conjured up in her mind, only to die stillborn as another thought succeeded it. Kefi's claws must have dug deep into Steel's flesh to cause such noticeable damage.

'You ought to get the wound dressed before infection sets in,' she advised him sternly.

'*Endaxi*!'

Unaware of the meaning of the short, sharp expletive delivered in a husky growl, Ginny started back in dismay. Alarm and astonishment rippled down her spine as with an easy movement Steel crossed his arms to seize the bottom of his shirt, hauling it over his head to reveal his naked back, demerara-brown, smoothly muscled and unblemished save for the deep, angry clawmarks on one shoulder-blade.

'Thanks,' he said laconically. 'I really appreciate your offer.'

Ginny's hand tightened round the coffee-jar. Had his misinterpretation of her counsel been deliberate or was the innocent look he turned on her as guileless as it appeared?

Almost certainly the former option, she decided, determined not to react to his subtle provocation. Besides, although the last thing she wanted to do was to touch the enticing golden skin presented for her attention, heaven alone knew where the little cat had been foraging for itself. She could hardly refuse to administer treatment to its unwilling saviour, could she?

'My pleasure,' she murmured ironically, replacing the coffee-jar on the shelf with a steady hand.

Steel sat motionless, elbows on the breakfast-bar, chin resting in cupped hands, while she set about the task she'd thoughtlessly imposed on herself. Hopefully, if he was aware of the way her fingers trembled, he wouldn't realise it was the feel of his bare skin beneath them that made her touch so uncertain.

It was a good thing he couldn't see her face, she thought as, fascinated by the way his dense, wavy hair lay in dark tendrils on the bowed column of his neck, she allowed her gaze to linger on it before dropping it in unwilling admiration to the powerful deltoid muscles of his shoulders.

Bathed and patted dry, the scratched area was improved but still inflamed. A touch of antiseptic cream and a plaster and her job would be done.

'There...' She stepped away from him, capping the tube of ointment, instilling an impersonal briskness into her voice. 'You can get dressed again, and I hope your tet jabs are up to date.'

'Everything about me is up to date, Ginny.' Released from her ministrations, he was on his feet in an instant, towering above her, forcing on to her the realisation of just how small her father's kitchen was.

Slowly biting her lip, she stayed a mild attack of claustrophobia, saying brightly, 'Go into the sitting-room and I'll bring your coffee in...'

He moved, and for a split-second she actually supposed he was going to obey her. Too late she realised her mistake, her breath sharpening as he paused beside her to lower his head and drop a light kiss on her mouth before one word of protest could leave it.

As her legs seemed to lose their power of support, the air between them was suddenly static and she staggered slightly, raising her hands in an automatic response to regain her balance, finding Steel's strong shoulders a ready support. His reaction was instantaneous. Bare arms slid round her body in automatic response, easing her into closer contact with his commanding frame.

For one indulgent moment Ginny found herself relaxing in the perilous harbour that surrounded her, comforted by the physical nearness of another human being. Then, as the lean, hard power of Steel's body trespassed too intimately for her peace of mind, she was shocked back to her senses.

'Steel...' She pushed urgently but vainly against the warm wall of his naked chest, raising her chin defiantly as she tried to arch away from him. 'Steel!' It was a desperate cry for release as he looked down lazily, uncomprehendingly, through lowered lashes at her upturned face.

'That was only a thank-you kiss, Ginny.' His deep-timbred voice made her catch her breath as his slanting gaze denied her the reprieve she begged. 'But this one isn't...'

It was like nothing she had ever experienced before as his predatory mouth flirted with her soft lips, seducing them with a complete masculine dominance, subjugating her half-hearted opposition until her arms unconsciously sought harbour around his neck and she melted against him. In his warm embrace her resistance melted, a shocking elation storming through her blood like a cyclone, sweeping away her reservations, leaving her breathless and trembling as he took sweet toll of her helplessness.

'Ginny...?' His breath was warm on her face as he eased the assault on her senses, easing his mouth from hers to trail his heated lips across her cheek.

Shocked, she heard and understood the question he was asking. Like a glass of iced water flung into her face, it dispelled her lethargy. With a moan of distress she tore herself from his arms and he let her go, the invitation still smouldering in the depths of his dark eyes as he watched her struggle to gain control over her responses.

'How dare you abuse my hospitality like this?' Anger at her own behaviour spilled over into accusation. Touched by a terrible comprehension, she knew that nothing in her life could ever be quite the same again. 'Just because I offered you coffee it didn't mean I was inviting you to...' Her voice faltered as, impaled by his steady glance, she found herself at a loss for words to describe the enormity of his digression.

'Kiss you?' He finished the sentence for her, demeaning her righteous indignation, dismissing her protest with a wry twist of his predatory mouth. 'That's all it was, Ginny. Just a kiss. And as for invitation...' He paused just long enough to allow her to perceive the glint of humour behind his thickly lashed eyes. 'You didn't seem to object the other night.'

Trust him to bring up the most embarrassing moment of her life until a few moments ago!

'When I was too exhausted and miserable to care what happened to me?' she demanded acidly. 'You found that encouraging?'

'Intriguing.' A narrow smile turned the corners of his mobile mouth—that warm, exciting mouth that had so recently laid claim to her own. Quickly she averted her eyes as he continued smoothly, 'I wondered if you respond so warmly to your fiancé's attentions.'

He'd handed her a lifeline which she was quick to grasp. 'How clever of you to guess I was missing him so badly,' she improvised swiftly. 'I'm afraid my reaction was automatic.' Something reckless stirring inside her persuaded her to disregard the dangerous gleam in his unremitting gaze, driving her to incautiousness. 'With my eyes shut I just pretended for a few moments that you were Howard.'

'Did you indeed?' He regarded her thoughtfully. 'Even though he'd abandoned you so brutally?'

'It wasn't like that!' Loyalty forced her to Howard's defence. 'He'd been looking forward to going to Rome for months. There was nothing he could do here...' Her voice tailed away as cold realisation chilled her blood. Steel was right. It had been like that. She could no longer deceive herself about Howard's priorities, or fail to be hurt by them.

'Of course it was, Ginny—and you know it.' Roughness lent an edge to his voice. 'You also know that Howard was the last person on your mind when you melted in my arms so passionately.'

Deprived of one excuse, she found another.

'You forced me!' Scarlet wedges flared in her cheeks, compounded by shame and embarrassment.

'Forced?' A sudden icy chill hung on the edge of his words as Steel's mouth tightened with displeasure. 'Persuaded is a better word, I think. I don't need to use force against women. If their favours aren't freely given, they can always be bought!'

The scathing retort made her flinch. Not mine, she thought, her eyes momentarily closing against his impaling scrutiny, his cool dismissal of the integrity of her sex filling her with untypical feminist fervour.

'Not every woman has a price,' she retorted angrily as he lounged back against the breakfast-bar. 'And we aren't all impressed by the cult of the aggressive, dominant male, either.' Infuriated by the lazy lift of his dark eyebrows which silently questioned her sincerity, she continued hotly, 'I can assure you that money couldn't buy anything from me that I wouldn't be prepared to give for nothing in the right circumstances.'

'And what would those be, hmm?' he asked with a deceptive softness which increased her misgivings by the second. 'Would making the money available for Sullivan's to appeal against the enforcement order that's threatening to put it out of business qualify?'

Gasping, as if the verbal blow below the belt had really winded her, Ginny made no attempt to hide the fiery resentment burning in her gaze as Steel turned away from her. Riveted by the nonchalance of his movements, she watched dumbly as he picked up his T-shirt, slinging it casually around his shoulders, before turning to face her again. The lift of his eyebrows coupled with his thin smile demanded that she answer his question.

'How dare you pry into our affairs?' Adrenalin coursed through her veins, reviving her power of speech, as she fought to control the rising tempo of her despair.

He shrugged. 'There's nothing confidential about enforcement notices. Details were published in the local newspaper yesterday. Besides, there's not much point in tearing down the evidence if you leave it in your waste-paper basket for anyone to see.'

'Dad doesn't know. He mustn't know.' Cursing her own carelessness, Ginny tightened her fists in frustration, the long oval fingernails biting into her soft palms.

'I'd be interested to know how you plan to prolong his ignorance. Time's hardly on your side, is it?' he enquired conversationally.

'I'll manage somehow!' Fighting down an urgent desire to slap the mocking expression from his handsome face, she lifted her chin arrogantly.

'Does that mean you're not interested in my offer of financial aid, then?'

'There's nothing you can offer me in which I'd be the least interested!'

It was an invitation for him to leave and for a fraction of a moment she thought he would have the grace to go. But obviously she'd underestimated the thickness of his skin.

'Wrong, Ginny!' His inflexible expression was unnerving. 'And what's more I can prove it!'

Her stomach muscles tensed as he closed in on her, forcing her to inhale her breath in a great sobbing gasp as one of his powerful hands gripped her chin, compelling her to look up into his darkly handsome face.

Damn her foolish tongue! She should have known better than to challenge him! Mesmerised by the dark power of his eyes, she found herself unable to move as his husky voice slewed disturbingly across her ears.

'I know just how desperate things are here. Not only the local council's threat to close down the warehouses because they claim they were originally designated as garages and their use for storage of goods constitutes illegal trading, or the fact that you're owed thousands of pounds by customers who can't or won't pay, but also that your main supplier, the foundation of Sullivan's previous success, is threatening to take away sole agency because of lack of guaranteed sales.' He paused, his expression enigmatic as Ginny felt despair seep through every cell of her body.

'But how could you know about Orchid? Who told you?'

'Wake up, Ginny!' His retort was rough. 'Sullivan's isn't existing in a vacuum. It's a highly competitive market. News travels fast.' His voice softened marginally, but his narrowed eyes remained merciless as he continued, 'In those circumstances I'd say I could offer Sullivan's quite a lot—not only financial aid to brief the best barrister available to contest the enforcement order, but also to install a modern computerised system to deal with credit control, and to employ at least two first-class salesmen to promote the products with the style they deserve.'

'No!' It was an anguished rebuttal of everything he suggested as Ginny found anger replacing her initial dejection. How dared he take advantage of her absence yesterday to pry into her father's affairs? 'Dad would never agree to put himself in the hands of a usurer!'

'But he would take a partner,' Steel suggested softly, only the cold, bright sparkle of his eyes betraying that he'd felt and resented her bitter thrust at his integrity.

'Never.' Vehemently she denied such a possibility, certain of her facts because her father had made his wishes clear to her time and time again in the past. It wasn't what she wanted, but he had insisted, and because she loved him she'd long ceased arguing with him. 'He's always told me he'd never consider taking a partner because Sullivan's always was and always would be a family concern. He wanted me to inherit everything.'

'Everything being nothing?' Firm hands tightened on her arms as she glanced away, defeated. 'Precisely, Ginny.' The note of triumph in his voice warmed its timbre. 'So you'll be delighted to know that I've talked to him and persuaded him to change his mind.'

'You visited my father in hospital?' Ginny's voice rose in disbelief. 'You intruded on a sick man——'

'Sick *friend*,' he corrected tersely. 'Leo and I are friends. He was delighted to see me. Physically sick he may be, but he was feeling a lot better by the time I left him. He's no fool, Ginny! The main cause of his ulcer was stress brought about by working a twenty-hour day in an effort to save what he sees as *your* inheritance. Believe me, he jumped at the opportunity of a cash infusion.'

Her mind spinning dizzily, Ginny took a step backwards and found herself released. 'You're lying,' she accused bitterly. 'There's nothing you could have told my father to convince him to sell you a share in Sullivan's.'

'Wrong!' he corrected her softly. 'There was one thing I could tell your father that not only changed his mind but brought a smile of joy to his pale face.'

'Which was?' She was trembling now, a strange primitive warning sounding in her brain.

Steel shrugged, a nonchalant movement of his broad shoulders. 'Why, that you and I were desperately in love and planned to marry just as soon as he was well enough to give you away.'

CHAPTER FIVE

GINNY'S mouth opened in shocked surprise, but it took several seconds before she could formulate any words, let alone a coherent sentence. 'But—but he'd never believe a lie like that! He knows I'm in love with Howard, that the two of us plan to get married...' she managed eventually.

'Certainly he knows that's what he was told,' Steel agreed coolly. 'But as he confided in me, he's never really believed that you'd go through with it. He thought that one day you'd realise what a dreadful mistake you'd be making. He was banking on the hope that by the time the two of you came back from Rome, having been forced into each other's company for hours on end, you'd have seen Howard for the self-centred chauvinist he really is.'

'Dad said that?' Ginny gasped, her mind in a whirl. Although her father had never actively opposed her professed intention to marry Howard she'd always had a niggling feeling that he didn't like the younger man, but she'd never guessed how deeply that dislike ran.

'So you can imagine how delighted he was when I explained you'd already seen the light, and that we'd been waiting for his complete recovery before putting him in the picture.'

'But we—you and I—are strangers!' Ginny's hands rose to her head, her fingers threading through her hair. Dear heavens, she must be having a nightmare!

'That could have been a problem, I admit.' Steel seemed singularly sanguine about the situation he'd engendered. 'Luckily, I was able to convince him we'd met six months ago at the catering fair in Birmingham, and our friendship had continued during your last term at Birmingham until it had ripened into love. After that it was just a matter of letting Howard down lightly, which you did before leaving Birmingham.'

Ginny gulped. 'You mean you told Dad I'd already cancelled the holiday before he was taken ill?'

'It seemed the most acceptable option.' He nodded. 'I told him you just hadn't got round to breaking the news to him.'

Hysteria rose and choked in Ginny's throat. 'How did you know I was at the exhibition?' she demanded. 'Guesswork? Or do you possess second sight?'

'No, just twenty-twenty vision.' He tossed her a superior smile. 'I had other things on my mind when I came down here the other night, but your face seemed familiar and it didn't take me too long to remember where I'd seen you before.'

'I *was* there,' Ginny recalled helplessly, 'but I never saw you—let alone spoke to you.'

'You were involved in a sale at the time, and I had other business to attend to, but the scarlet knitted jersey dress you were wearing left an imprint on my mind. If I hadn't had another appointment later that evening I would have asked you to have dinner with me.'

'And I would have refused!' she snapped back, making a mental note to donate the jersey dress to a charity shop. 'You're telling me Dad actually swallowed all that... that drivel?'

'Uh-huh! With gratifying eagerness.' His dark eyes laughed at her outraged face.

'Then the sooner he realises he's been taken for a fool the better!' Furiously she rounded on him. 'If you think for one moment that I'm going through with this absurd masquerade——'

'Oh, but you are, Ginny,' Steel's voice was harshly authoritative as he broke into her angry outburst, 'because it's the only chance you've got to put Sullivan's back on an even keel, and you know it as well as I do.'

'And what's in it for you?' she blazed.

'Oh, I have my motives,' he acknowledged blithely. 'But they're no concern of yours at the moment. All I require *you* to do is play the part of a rapturously happy, newly engaged girl.'

'And if I refuse?'

He shrugged. 'You'll be responsible for breaking Sullivan's back—and your father's heart!' He reached into his trouser pocket as Ginny's breath hissed in between her clenched teeth at the callousness of his retort. 'Just to add to the illusion, you'd better wear this.'

She stared as he flipped open the lid of a small jeweller's box to reveal a diamond and sapphire cluster ring, and the words he'd spoken to her in the Keys echoed in Ginny's mind. 'If you were my betrothed, Ginny, you'd most certainly wear my ring.'

'Here...' He took the ring from its velvet bed and placed it on the unresisting finger of her left hand. 'Hmm, not a bad fit.'

She stared down at the meaningless symbol, an emptiness behind her ribs where her heart should be. From their first encounter Steel Anastasi had realised she'd do anything to help her father, but when had he decided on this devious plot—and why?

'How long am I expected to act out this charade?' she asked tonelessly.

'Until it's served its purpose.' His tone warned her he didn't intend to be more explicit as he glanced down at the slim analogue watch which graced his sinewy wrist. 'And now I think it's time to introduce myself to the rest of the staff and put them in the picture.'

'I'll be right with you.' Glad of the chance to disperse by movement the build-up of tension which had knotted her muscles, Ginny started towards the door, only to find herself brought to a halt as Steel's arm snaked about her waist.

'Your presence isn't part of my plans, Ginny,' he told her gently—too gently. 'I'm quite capable of explaining the situation to them and I prefer to do it alone.'

'But I have to be there——'

'Correction. You have to be *here*, Ginny. Part of my agreement with Leo is that you're no longer concerned with the active running of the business.' He cast the eye of a predator around the room. 'I'm sure you can find plenty to occupy yourself with around the house. For a start Kefi would probably appreciate an introduction to his new quarters as well as something to eat. Then, no doubt, you'll want to visit your father and receive his blessing.'

'But...' she began heatedly, only to lapse into silence, her protest unspoken. Really she had no choice, she reflected sourly, furious at the way he was already destroying the carefully woven fabric of her life, but too aware of the lifeline he'd thrown her father to oppose his plan with the scorn it deserved.

'Until tonight, then, *agape mou*. But before I go I think a small rehearsal is in order to put a sparkle into your beautiful eyes and add a little conviction to your performance when you visit Leo.'

The small step she took to evade him as she read his intention was too little and too late as he closed the distance between them, his mouth seeking hers, his warm lips imprinting his physical superiority, sealing the terms of the bargain he'd forced on her. So why was what he had intended as a lesson giving her so much pleasure? Why was she feeling this warm, suffusing glow as his hands released her arms to imprison her body, sliding slowly, caressingly down her back?

Ginny had no answer to these questions as a deep shudder racked her from top to toe, wiping out all desire to oppose him, leaving her mouth free to welcome his kiss as it deepened to become a sweet, slow ravishment of her senses.

Instinctively her youthful body sought the complementary pattern of Steel's tough, masculine frame, the yawning ache she experienced telling her in the most frightening way possible that, despite her earlier conclusions, whatever she felt for Steel Anastasi it wasn't indifference.

It was Steel's soft groan that brought her back to her senses as he released her with startling abruptness, pushing her away from him as if contact with her had contaminated him.

The ache in her breasts was excruciating, but she dared not touch them in case she drew his attention to the prominence of the nipples shadowed beneath the form-fitting fabric of her blouse.

Shame and self-contempt fuelled her reaction as he turned on his heel and made for the front door.

'Get out of my house!' she yelled at his retreating back. 'I won't expose this thing for the pitiful sham it is, but you needn't think it gives you any right to come and go as you please. The less I see of you the better.'

'Oh, did I forget to tell you?' On the threshold he paused, studying her with knowing eyes, arrogant, self-willed and amusing himself by playing power games, using his lean, supple male body as an instrument of his pride and passion. 'Leo was very concerned about your living in the house alone—something about a spate of local burglaries, women being attacked in their homes at night. So I promised him I'd move in with you and protect you. I'll be bringing my things over later today.'

If she'd still had the coffee-cup in her hand, she'd have thrown it at his expensively clad shoulder-blades! Instead Ginny contented herself with slamming the door behind him, before making her way back to the living-room and casting herself down on one of the comfortable leather-covered armchairs, feeling as if she'd been plucked from the security of a familiar world and flung, fettered, into a bizarre and alien landscape.

At least, she consoled herself, thankful though she was that a rescue operation had been mounted, she owed Steel nothing in terms of gratitude, for plunging her into a scenario where both the script and the nature of her co-actor were unknown quantities.

Little wonder he'd barred her from going to the office. Not that she'd the slightest intention of obeying his per-emptory instructions! Cathy and Duncan would be eager to see her and congratulate her on her unexpected en-gagement and she'd no intention of disappointing them.

Still, it might be preferable to give them time to recover from the series of shocks Steel was about to deliver...

She spent the next hour trying to keep her mind occupied by tidying the house, although, since her mother's death from meningitis shortly after her own fourth birthday, Leo had taken over the reins of household management with an iron determination, and there was little for her to do.

He was a father in a million—loving, tolerant and loyal, and the special closeness which they shared defied the so-called generation gap, despite the fact that he'd been forty-three when she'd been born. She'd make any sacrifice for him, she acknowledged fiercely, running the vacuum cleaner over the fitted carpets, even to agreeing to make up the bed in the spare room for his new partner, if that was going to put his mind at rest about her and hasten his recovery. Although how he would react when he realised how badly he'd been duped... Resolutely Ginny forced her mind away from that problem. Time enough to face it when Steel Anastasi had achieved his own ends and Sullivan's was thriving once more.

It was just before midday when she stalked across the yard and thrust open the office door, prepared to do battle with Steel if necessary, but there was no sign of him as Cathy leaped to her feet and came swiftly across to embrace her.

'Ginny, my dear! What marvellous news!' The older woman's eyes filled with tears, whether because of the company's reprieve or what she saw as Ginny's newly found happiness was difficult for the latter to determine. 'And such a surprise!' If there was the slightest hint of remonstrance in Cathy's voice, Ginny managed to ignore it.

'Yes, isn't it?' she returned brightly. 'I can hardly believe it myself.'

She managed to conjure up a bright smile as Cathy released her and Duncan came towards her to grasp her hand in congratulation, while Leo's secretary continued enthusiastically, 'Of course, I understand why you were waiting for Leo to recover before announcing it publicly. How ironic that unknowingly he forced your hand by refusing to accept financial help from the very man who turned out to be your fiancé! I would have loved to have seen his face when Mr Anastasi—Steel—told him!'

'I would have liked to have been there myself,' Ginny said, unable to restrain the tinge of acid which sharpened the comment. So Steel had already made his glib explanations, and obviously with a good amount of persuasive charm! It was galling to have to recognise the possibility that both Cathy and Duncan had known her so-called fiancé a great deal longer than she had!

'I take it Steel's put both of you completely in the picture?' she added drily.

'You take it quite correctly, sweetheart.'

She hadn't heard his approach. The first intimation of his presence was when his deep, warm voice hit her ears. Spinning round to face him, lifting her chin aggressively, she dared him to comment adversely on her presence.

'I thought you were going to visit your father this morning?' He came to her side, sliding his arm around her shoulders, moving his fingers insidiously against the warm flesh of her upper arm.

'I am, darling.' She gave him a taut smile. 'I thought I'd just call in here to see if Cathy needs a hand with anything.'

'No.' Smoothly and quickly he declined her offer. 'I have everything under control. What Sullivan's needs now is more *professional* help and that's what I'm organising at the moment.' The smile he cast her was friendly enough, but the dark eyes held a warning. 'Besides, I'm using Leo's desk myself so there's no room for you.' He glanced briefly at his watch. 'Why don't you run along to the hospital now, darling? I imagine your father has a hundred and one questions to ask you. And afterwards you could do some shopping for your trousseau. You're not a librarian any more, Ginny, so there's no reason why you should continue to dress like one, is there?'

Damn him for his patronising rebuke!

'But...' she began to protest, only to falter as the bright sparkle of his dark eyes reminded her of the other occupants of the room and the need to phrase her objections with care.

'Don't worry about getting lunch,' Steel interjected smoothly. 'I've got a lot to do today so we can have a nice long chat over dinner tonight instead.'

Firmly he propelled her towards the door, ushering her through it and continuing to march her out of earshot before releasing her.

'I thought I told you there's no room for amateurs in this organisation.' His expression held a mocking glint which sent her temper soaring. 'I don't enjoy being thwarted, Ginny.'

'And I don't enjoy being ordered about like a child!' She gave him a hostile glare. 'You may have managed to fool my father into believing you're some kind of hero, but I know just how devious you are and I don't trust you! If I want to visit the office to keep an eye on what you're doing then I will, and nothing you can say will prevent it!'

Determined to have the last word, she turned on her heel, her body taut with anger.

'*Say* no! *Do* yes!'

Steel's retort hit her ears as she felt herself being swept off her feet to be hoisted unceremoniously over his shoulder in what she recognised as a superbly executed fireman's lift.

Anger, outrage and a touch of fear mingled in her startled cry.

'Put me down, you brute!' Beating furious fists against his powerful back, she struggled fruitlessly as he strode across the yard towards the back entrance into the house.

Mortified lest the neighbours should witness her undignified arrival, her only consolation being that she was wearing jeans and not a skirt, she bit back further verbal recriminations until he'd neatly located her key in the back pocket of her jeans and admitted them both into the house.

'Steel, put me down!' Her voice rose wildly as, still without speaking, he mounted the stairs, choosing a room at random and footing it open. A grunt of satisfaction greeted the sight of Leo's double bed and he dropped her, with little regard for her dignity, on to its softness.

His breathing laboured, a faint touch of pink colouring his tanned cheekbones, he remained standing over her, staring down, his contemplation unnerving.

Ginny swallowed miserably, appalled by the warring emotions which stirred inside her, engendering a physical response which was frightening in its intensity and implication. Her defiance, Steel's irritation at it, coupled with the intimate contact of their bodies, had acted as a powerful aphrodisiac and not only on the man whose dark face was subtly changed by the release of the powerful male hormones which had primed his arrogant masculine anatomy, but, shamefully, on her own less predatory body.

She couldn't speak; only her widened eyes pleaded with him, silently begging him not to touch her, as the words of abuse she'd been rehearsing for use at her moment of freedom remained unuttered.

When Steel did move it was to reach out a hand towards her with a strangely gentle gesture, to push the tumbled mass of hair back from her face, before trailing his fingers down to touch her mouth, which trembled against their restrained caress.

'Don't fight me, Ginny. We're both on the same side.'

'Are we?' A small pulse beat hard in her throat, and she was painfully aware that Steel knew the extent of the punishment he had inflicted on her. 'If this is how you treat your allies, what happens to your enemies?'

'Behave yourself and you needn't worry about that.' His smile flashed briefly, dazzling against the smooth olive tan of his face. 'And don't forget to give Leo my love.'

It was early afternoon before she felt composed enough to visit her father. In the interim period she'd rehearsed the role into which she'd been cast. There was no way she could let Leo guess that her 'engagement' to Steel was anything but genuine, although she felt sick at the thought of deceiving him. Clearly he thought highly of the man who had tricked him into believing that he was about to become his son-in-law.

Strange, she mused, as she parked the Renault in the hospital car park, because generally Leo Sullivan was an excellent judge of character. Slipping the parking receipt inside her windscreen, she shook her head in despair. The stress which had resulted in his collapsing must have confused his normal ability to discern the false from the genuine.

Glad that years of paying for private medical insurance had assured her father the comparative luxury of an amenity room—with its additional benefit of open visiting hours—in the local hospital, she drew a deep breath before knocking on the door and entering.

'Ginny, my dear!' He was still attached to a drip, but Leo Sullivan's smile belied his condition. 'It's the most marvellous news I've had in years—and before you can say anything I want you to know that Steel has explained everything to me, and I quite understand your previous reticence.' He shook his head, reaching out to clasp her hand as she seated herself on the bed. 'To be honest, I never thought Howard was the right man for you, but it wasn't for me to criticise your choice.'

'And you fully approve of Steel?' If there was an edge of irony to the question she managed to conceal it.

'Absolutely. He and I have known each other for a couple of years, ever since he started buying up non-profitable restaurants, refurbishing them and turning them into successful businesses.' He squeezed her hand. 'Not bad for a young man who turned his back on his home and family at the age of eighteen to make his own destiny, eh?' He sighed, not waiting for her answer. Not that one was forthcoming, Ginny accorded silently as she digested the only information she had to date about Steel's background. 'To be honest with you, darling, Sullivan's has been going through a very rocky patch these last six months and at times I wondered if I'd be able to keep it going. Now at last I can relax, knowing that both your future and that of the company are in safe hands.'

'Yes, of course you can, Dad!' What else could she have said? 'All you've got to do now is get better as soon as you can so you can lead me down the aisle.'

She hated lying to him, yet it was worth it to see the contentment soften the gaunt lines of his face. When the time came to disillusion him he'd forgive her, she was sure, and she'd be free to take up her life where she'd left it, perhaps even take the postgraduate course in Librarianship she had planned. Her life would go on as before...except for Howard...Howard would never forgive her for taking part in this farce, even if that was what she wanted; and since the events of the past days she was no longer sure what she did want.

Masking her inner qualms, she stayed for an hour, chattering about this and that, discussing the latest news in the papers, until she saw the signs of tiredness etch their lines on her father's face and knew it was time to leave.

She spent the next few hours driving around the countryside in an effort to come to terms with the incredible events which had shattered the even pattern of her life, tearing it asunder, flinging the pieces into free fall, to leave them swirling in a maelstrom of unexplained purpose.

At the centre of her dilemma stood Steel Anastasi, whose heart was doubtless as black as the soft hair which clung to the skull of his handsome head. Because he must want an interest in Sullivan's badly, very badly indeed if he was prepared to go to such lengths to get it!

She'd covered a greater mileage than she'd realised, so that it was growing dusk when she drew up outside the house to discover the Lotus Carlton neatly parked on the forecourt. Lights gleaming behind the curtained windows told their own story.

'What the blazes do you think you're playing at?' As Steel came to greet her she flung the question at him, her rebellious emotions out of hand as she stepped across the threshold, her car keys gripped in fingers which shook with anger.

'My line, I think, darling.' His expression bordered on mockery as he surveyed her furious face. 'I didn't throw a brick through the window to gain access, if that's what's worrying you. I still have the key I obtained this morning—remember?'

Yes, she did remember and the recollection suffused her face with a wave of colour.

'Besides, any explanation required has to come from you. Where have you been, Ginny?'

'Out.' The insolence in her voice was barely concealed. 'Why? Were you expecting me to provide your dinner as well as a bed for the night?'

'Since your father has cast me in the role of chaperon, I was expecting the courtesy of being informed about your whereabouts.' His coldly critical glance swung over her. 'I checked at the hospital and was told you'd left hours earlier.'

'So——' she shrugged '—I went for a drive. I had things to think about.' Her breath came raggedly in impotent anger, her grey eyes blazing as they swept across his implacable face. 'Do you intend to keep me in purdah?'

'Suppress your temper by judicial punishment while I teach you the arts of pleasuring a man?' His smile was coolly calculating, the glint in his dark eyes echoing the promise of retribution he had suggested. 'What a tempting possibility, Ginny, one well worth considering if I hadn't promised your father I'd protect rather than chastise you, although...' he paused, regarding her through assessing eyes, while the breath burned in her throat '... the two may not be mutually exclusive. Have you eaten?'

'Not since lunch.' Relieved that he had apparently abandoned his previous belligerent stance, she forced herself to give him a civil answer. 'I don't have much appetite.'

'Hmm. I'd offer to take you out for a meal, but something tells me that in your present mood we might end up being thrown out for creating a disturbance. So what do you say to a take-away?'

Ginny made an indifferent movement with her shoulders. Now her initial spurt of anger had abated, common sense told her there was no point in provoking him further. She was stuck with a man who was determined to have his own way regardless of anyone or anything. A shiver laced her spine with sudden chill. What if that way included an even closer relationship than a mock-engagement suggested? No, her fears savoured too much of melodrama. No normal man played games like that. On the other hand, what was normal about a man who admittedly thought that every woman had her price?

CHAPTER SIX

I COULD phone for a pizza,' Ginny offered coldly.

'Fine.' Steel indicated the telephone by her side. 'I'll be in the sitting-room when you've finished.'

The call took only a few seconds but, determined not to be ordered about in her own home, Ginny decided to have a quick shower and change her clothes before rejoining her uninvited house guest.

The memory of his earlier uncalled-for and probably slanderous gibe concerning her clothes had her searching through her wardrobe for something more sophisticated to wear.

Choosing a simple burnt-orange cotton and Lycra shift dress, its fashionably short skirt showing off her long, slender legs to advantage, she slipped her nyloned feet into high-heeled taupe sandals. If nothing else, the added stature should give her much needed confidence, although she'd still be several inches short of seeing eye-to-eye with Steel—literally as well as metaphorically.

'You look as if you need this.' As she joined him, Steel turned from the drinks cabinet, offering her one of Leo's champagne flutes filled to the brim with sparkling wine. The dark green bottle on the table, its wired cork carelessly abandoned, told its own story.

'Champagne? Isn't that a little ostentatious?' She lifted what she hoped was a supercilious eyebrow. Steel might have raided her father's glass cabinet, but she was certain Leo's limited alcohol stock hadn't contained champagne.

77

'I prefer the word traditional.' He flashed her an insincere smile. 'What better way to celebrate Sullivan's reprieve and our betrothal?'

'I'll drink to the former.' She took the glass from him. Hopefully the contents would do something to calm her jangling nerves! 'Cheers!' She tossed the heady liquid down her throat with total disregard for its quality or its effervescent effect. It was a bad error of judgement, but when she'd finished gasping and managed to draw a coherent breath again she held out her glass for a refill, her head held high, her gaze imperious.

Solemnly Steel obliged her. Glowering into the pale golden depths, without a word of thanks, she moved into the attack.

'You must want an interest in Sullivan's pretty badly if you're prepared to go to such extremes to get a foothold in it,' she accused him bitingly, voicing her darkest suspicions.

'Now, why did I think you'd be on your knees thanking me for mounting a last-hour rescue, hmm?' Her allegation seemed to amuse him. Selecting another glass, he poured himself a generous measure of wine before strolling across the room to lounge down on the comfortable couch, totally at ease, long legs stretched out in front of him.

'Because you think I enjoy being manipulated?' She took a deep, steadying breath. 'Because it's never occurred to you that we could manage without your interference?' His cynical expression, confirming that the idea had never entered his brain, stung her to further excess. 'Howard has savings!' she cried rashly. 'He would have loaned us the money to brief a barrister——'

'Wishful thinking, sweetheart.' He regarded her coolly as she flinched from the sardonically mouthed endearment. 'A man who goes away and leaves the woman he's supposed to love in a situation like this one isn't going to risk his savings to rescue her father from bankruptcy. Leo knows it and you know it. Even to an outsider like myself it's clear that the interests of you and your father are among Howard's lowest priorities.'

Hurtful though it was, a small voice inside Ginny told her Steel's rough diagnosis was true, but she wasn't prepared to admit it aloud.

'As you say,' she retorted icily. 'To an *outsider* like you.'

'Not any more, Ginny.' He was on his feet swift as a cheetah, and as powerful, standing in front of her, taking the glass from her hand and placing it on the table beside her. 'You forget I'm Leo Sullivan's future son-in-law and that makes me very much of an *insider*.'

'In name only! I want to know the truth, Steel.' Every line of her taut body spoke defiance. 'What's in it for you?'

'Apart from teaching the teacher a lesson about the dangers of neglect?' Humour shimmered in the sable depths of his eyes. 'It's how I earn my living. Rescue and resuscitation. Taking the weak and faltering and returning it to full, abundant health. It's a challenge, Ginny.' His voice held a note of impatience. 'Sullivan's is handling first-class merchandise with plenty of potential for future expansion. Also, it's in my own interests to keep a good product available for my own businesses. What would you have preferred me to do? Accept Leo's decision to go on alone? I told you—I regard him as a friend. You know how he felt. It was *you*, Ginny. What he saw as your interests which were going to put the last nail in the coffin.'

He stood there gazing down at her, wholly cool and collected, his eyes resting sardonically on her anguished face, while she faltered, aware that his cool analysis of the situation was partly responsible for her surging despair.

'If you want to go back to the hospital and disillusion him I can't stop you, but I suggest you think seriously about his reaction.' He hammered his point home relentlessly.

Ginny glared at him with reproachful eyes, her fingers twisting round the graceful fluted glass. 'You know perfectly well that I can't deny it now, not after he was so— so...'

'Delighted is the word I think you're looking for,' Steel suggested gravely.

To her relief a sharp ring at the doorbell robbed her of the necessity to reply. Glad to escape, she dashed from the room to take delivery of the large pizza she'd ordered. Carrying it directly to the kitchen, she warmed two plates quickly beneath the hot-water tap as she selected knives, forks and table napkins, and her thoughts drifted back to the first time she'd seen Howard.

They'd met at an inter-college tennis match during her second year at university. His blond good looks had drawn the attention of several of her female friends. How flattered she'd been when he'd shown an interest in her! Always available when he needed a female companion, always understanding when he broke dates because some other engagement had cropped up.

She reached for a tea-towel to dry the warm plates. It had been an easy, tolerant relationship, even if she had sometimes wished he'd treat her more as an irresistible female than an accommodating sister! But she'd told herself that his apparent coolness was because he respected her, and that was how she wanted it.

Not for Ginette Sullivan the passionate love-affairs which ended traumatically in tears and despair. Howard was dependable. Resolutely she abandoned the word dull which flashed for a treacherous moment in her consciousness. Their relationship had matured gradually, their twosome accepted by their friends as a stable association which would eventually lead to marriage.

Continuing to move the cloth across plates which were already dry, she sighed. Howard had never actually proposed to her. They'd simply drifted into a situation where marriage seemed the obvious long-term outcome—after Howard got the headmastership he craved. It was a tacit understanding between them. If he had reservations about her father being in trade he rarely let them surface. On the contrary, he'd let her know on numerous occasions how suitable a wife she'd make for him, with her pleasant appearance and good but not outstanding degree in a 'suitable' subject.

Sure, she admitted to herself, their union wouldn't have been a spectacular, continuing display of fireworks. Not for Howard and her the switchback ride of passion and pain that marred so many marriages. They would have been a law-abiding, conformist couple, sharing mutual respect, providing an excellent example to the boys in Howard's school. Who wanted fireworks anyway?

She was thinking in the past tense. Putting the plates on a tray, carefully she cut the pizza into two portions. Howard was out of her life for good. Not only because he would be outraged by her part in Steel's conspiracy, but because she had at last recognised the painful truth. There were many qualities she admired in Howard, but she didn't love him—something she would never admit to Steel Anastasi, who had acted as the brutal catalyst in revealing it.

The arrogant destroyer of her dreams had resumed his seat by the time she returned to the living-room, her expression carefully controlled to conceal the trauma of her recent realisation. Springing to his feet, he relieved her of the tray.

'Mmm, delicious.' He smiled his approval. 'But I think you've overestimated my appetite.' His gaze swept over the way she'd divided the pizza as she placed his large portion on the low coffee-table in front of the settee.

'I doubt it,' she returned drily, adding quickly as she saw from the glint in his eyes that he'd found a double meaning to her reply, 'I'm not very hungry myself. Finding myself engaged to marry two men at the same time seems to have destroyed my appetite.'

'That's easily resolved.' He spread the napkin across his knees, slicing a portion of pizza and picking it up in his fingers. 'Phone Howard in Rome and tell him he's a free man again.' Lifting the slice to his mouth, he bit sharply into it with strong white teeth, as if he was symbolically snapping off Howard's head, she thought uncharitably.

'I can't!' she protested, irritated anew by his lack of feeling. 'It's not the kind of news one breaks over the phone.'

'You can and will, Ginny.' A hard core of determination deepened the timbre of his voice. 'If you don't then I will, because Leo believes you've already told him. Besides, it's not in my nature to share a woman.'

'Since the question of "sharing" me doesn't actually arise, I consider it's up to me to decide how and when I bring Howard up to date with events.' She glared her displeasure at the imperturbable countenance opposite her. 'For pity's sake, Steel—I've had just about enough of your interference and I resent being referred to as if I were a pizza!'

'Hot, tasty, succulent…to be enjoyed on the premises or taken away and appreciated at leisure?' His lips twisted into a cynical smile. 'It wasn't what I had in mind, but I see the possibilities now you've pointed them out.'

'It's not a joke.' A faint thread of hysteria raised the pitch of Ginny's voice. 'Just because you've forced me into a false position you needn't think it gives you any right to give me orders or to expect me to obey them.'

Calmly and meticulously Steel wiped his hands on the napkin as she watched him, heart thumping, her own small portion of food left untasted.

'Oh, I don't know…' His eyes met hers disparagingly. 'Since I've agreed to invest a six-figure sum of money into what is at the moment a very shaky concern, I consider I've purchased every right to do just that.'

'You're talking drachmas, of course?' she returned instantly, the beat of her heart intensifying in anticipation of his reply.

'No. Not drachmas, not US dollars—pounds sterling.'

'But…' she began, wanting desperately to disbelieve him. In sterling the scale of investment was enormous,

ridiculous. He had to be lying, trying to impress her...
'We only need a few thousand to pay legal costs...'

'Wake up, Ginny!' Derision and sympathy mingled in
his expression as he met and held her wide-eyed gaze.
'You may have led most of your adult life in the unreal
halls of academia, but even you can't be that naïve. You
know as well as I do that there's far more to be done to
ensure Sullivan's salvation than fighting petty bu-
reaucracy.' He made an impatient gesture with one hand.
'The company needs a complete overhaul including the
installation of an efficient computer system to deal with
the whole spectrum of the business from purchasing
through invoicing to stock control—and that costs
money, real money.'

Of course he was right. It was the conclusion she
herself had reached during the previous four days. But
the sum he was proposing to invest, even at the lowest
possible six-figure level, was staggering. No wonder Leo
had initially refused it, with all the implications it
contained.

Her throat felt raw, a suffocating sensation tightening
her gullet for which her unwise draught of champagne
couldn't be held totally responsible.

'So you see,' Steel was continuing calmly, 'we can't
risk your errant boyfriend returning and expecting to
take up his relationship with you where he dropped it.'

'Do you make a habit of going around destroying
people's lives?' Her breath came irregularly as impotent
anger tightened her diaphragm. She didn't love
Howard—but supposing she had?

'Transforming perhaps would be a better word,' Steel
corrected her cheerfully. 'But I shouldn't shed too many
tears on Howard's behalf. If he's only half the man I

suspect he is, he'll manage to cope quite well with your desertion.'

The callous comment wasn't intended as a compliment to Howard's character and she wasn't fooled into believing that Leo's new partner cared a damn about the other man's feelings.

'And what about my feelings? Don't they count for anything at all?' she demanded.

'Isn't that the question you should have asked Howard when he decided to go on holiday without you?' he retorted briskly. 'Forget him, Ginny. I doubt he's spending much time thinking of you while he's enjoying the pleasures of Italy.' He paused to cast discerning eyes over her tautly held figure. 'Besides, I can't have you dragging any emotional encumbrances with you when I present you to my own father as my potential bride.'

Helplessly Ginny returned his regard, feeling herself drifting further and further out of her depth, as she tried to make sense of his reply. 'Your father?' she said at last, weakly.

'You supposed I didn't have one?' His mouth curled derisively. 'Relax! It's not going to be that difficult! All you have to do is smile prettily when I introduce you, and act like a girl who's about to marry into one of the wealthiest Greek families since Onassis. Sparkle the way women do when they find they've got their hands on a rich man's wallet!'

Millionaires? He was talking millionaires? She stared at him aghast, her mind racing, remembering at last why the name Anastasi had seemed familiar. It was a name which appeared regularly in the City pages of the financial press—and it explained several things about

Steel Anastasi which had puzzled her, not the least being his high-handed way of dealing with people and events.

'Pandelis Anastasi,' she said flatly, cursing herself for not having realised earlier. 'Pandelis Anastasi, the hotel and property magnate, is your father?'

'You're telling me that you've only just worked that out?'

She felt her mouth drop open in shock as his sarcastic tone confirmed her inference, and had to make a concerted effort to stop gaping. 'Of course I've heard of Pandelis Anastasi—who hasn't? But it's a common enough Greek surname, isn't it? I mean, I assumed——'

'That my beginnings were more humble?' He lifted a dark eyebrow.

'Well, yes,' she admitted, refusing to be quelled by his patronising smile. 'It's not often we get a millionaire's son throwing his weight around in our warehouse.' But she might have guessed. The Lotus Carlton, the designer suit, the sheer arrogance of the man. He'd been as out of place in Sullivan's yard as a thoroughbred racehorse on a caravan site. Ginny chewed on her lower lip, chagrined that she had been so immersed in her own problems at that first meeting that her customary powers of deduction had deserted her. 'But the Keys of Corfu isn't owned by Anastasi Holdings! My father's been trying to get their custom for ages without success.'

'So you aren't completely ignorant of what's been happening while you've been enjoying yourself elsewhere.' He cast her a disparaging glance from needle-sharp eyes. 'My business interests are totally independent of my father's. I have no connections with Anastasi Holdings. Neither do I desire any.'

'So what is this all about?' Ginny demanded, frustration sharpening her tone. 'And even more to the point—why choose me? I'd have thought there'd be enough women already in your life able and willing to put on a performance for you, without your having to lay out good money to buy one!'

'Plenty lining up to share my bed.' Steel nodded complacently, apparently totally undisturbed by her reaction. 'But unfortunately none suitable for my purpose.'

'Which is?' Watching while he cut himself another wedge of pizza, she found her legs suddenly too weak to support her. Sinking down into the refuge of the facing armchair, she awaited his explanation. She'd always known that there was more to Steel's apparent benevolence to a friend in need than a kindly gesture.

He was a businessman, not a philanthropist. She'd been able to handle her suspicions while she'd believed his financial interest to be minimal, but at the level of investment he'd claimed he would be looking for a higher return than Sullivan's—even with a vital cash transfusion administered—could ever provide. Now, she surmised grimly, she was about to discover the full price she was being asked to pay.

Steel took his time before answering, finishing his pizza, ignoring—if he was aware of it—the impatient drumming of her fingers on the leather beneath her hands.

Just when she thought she'd explode with frustration, he wiped his hands once more and leaned back. Relaxed and replete, he rewarded her with a smile. The kind of smile a bank manager might give when refusing to extend an overdraft, she decided, her nerves stretched to breaking-point.

'I intend to thwart the plans my father is busy building on the false premise that he can rely on my dutiful compliance to bail him out of trouble, regardless of personal cost to myself.'

Whatever she'd expected, it wasn't the casual announcement of intention to defy paternal demands, unreasonable though they seemed. She frowned, casting her mind back to her last visit to the hospital. 'My father mentioned something about your turning your back on home and family when you were younger...'

Steel's brilliant gaze burned into her questioning face. 'A breach in our relationship Pandelis chooses to ignore. His long association with *putanas* has left him under the impression that everyone can be bought if the price is right. I don't question his opinion where women are concerned, but my integrity isn't for sale.'

Life must have dealt him a very painful blow at a vulnerable age for him to evince such cynicism, Ginny determined, staring back at the adamantine set of his features, wishing she knew more about his background.

Slowly she shook her head, forcing herself to meet the challenge in his fierce expression. 'You're refusing to cooperate with your father because of something that happened several years ago?' she asked tentatively.

'Fifteen years ago, to be precise. I was seventeen.' Tersely he broke the expectant silence, a small muscle in his temple twitching as he continued without any other show of emotion, 'Her name was Louli. She was several years older than I, very beautiful, very exciting and very, very good in bed.' He paused reminiscently, a bright self-mockery twisting the corners of his mouth. 'I was young, arrogant and I fancied myself deeply in love. I wanted to marry her—that is, until the day I came across her and my father in circumstances which left no possible doubt as to the intimacy of their relationship.'

'Oh!' Try as she might Ginny couldn't prevent the shocked exclamation bursting from her lips as she visualised the sordid scene. It wasn't difficult to imagine Steel's shock and disillusionment.

Ignoring her interruption, he continued calmly, 'Louli burst into tears, but Pandelis laughed. He told me she'd been his mistress for two years and he'd actually paid her to initiate me into the rites of what he liked to term love.'

Coolly cynical now, his narrowed eyes lingered on Ginny's appalled face. 'You're not laughing? Don't you find it an amusing story?'

He was inviting her to smile, to ridicule the naïveté and agony of the young man he'd once been, but she found nothing humorous in his exposure of a side of his nature still raw with the memory of that humiliating dénouement.

He was waiting, head slanted a little to one side, for her reply. She had to make some kind of response, knowing he wouldn't want pity or commiseration. Instinct told her that even at the tender age of seventeen he would have rejected those sentiments. How much more so now, when maturity had honed his character to the fine, sharp edge which was so aptly matched by his name?

'I would think,' she began hesitantly, watching the dark pools of his eyes for any sign that she was trespassing too dangerously, 'that whatever part your father played in events Louli would never have agreed to become your lover unless—unless she cared very much for you. I mean, it's possible, isn't it?' she persevered as he remained silent. She was in deep water and he wasn't going to throw her a lifebelt. He was just sitting there, keen, penetrating eyes scorching into her soul, forcing her breathing to quicken defensively. 'I mean...' She floundered miserably, seeking some way to ameliorate his wounded pride. 'I mean, she could probably see and love in you the same attributes which had attracted her to your father—otherwise whatever rewards your father offered her she wouldn't have been able to... to...'

'Have sex with me?' Steel laughed harshly as she faltered to a halt, mocking his own youthful ingenuousness. 'How truly naïve you are, Ginny! Sex is merely a function of the body, an appetite which demands appeasing, a thirst which insists on being quenched, a trick of nature which assures the continuation of the human species.'

He gave a short bark of laughter. 'Anyway I left home, took myself out of college and worked in the tourist tavernas, saving every drachma I could to support myself during my national service. When that was over I went back to catering—saved until I could afford to buy my own taverna—and the rest, as they say, is history. I have restaurants in every free capital in Europe.'

'And Louli?' Ginny asked softly.

He laughed. 'A year after I'd left home Pandelis threw her out, having found himself a young lady who wasn't going to settle for anything less than marriage. By then he'd been a widower for ten years and doubtless his stamina was waning, if not his appetite, and he was looking for something more permanent than the endless parade of women who'd taken my mother's place.'

Sensitive enough to realise he didn't want to know anything about the rush of pity which had assailed her heart, Ginny stared down silently at her empty glass as he continued easily, 'It took five years before I realised Pandelis had taught me a lesson far more valuable than mere sexual proficiency.' His voice was casual now, conversational. 'And that is that every woman does have her price. Oh, some hold out longer than others, some are more grasping than others, some want money or jewellery, others public acclaim or social standing, a high profile in business. Ambition, Ginny.' He rose to his feet, crumpling his napkin and leaving it on the table. 'That's an emotion I can respect, a currency I can deal in, but the terms are mine and the rewards I reap must justify my efforts.'

Ginny gazed at him, relieved that he appeared to be bringing their meeting to an end, as her mind groped for something suitably non-committal to say. 'At least you're honest about your attitude.'

He nodded. 'That way no one gets hurt.'

'Except your father?' Bewildered, she shook her head. 'You still haven't explained why pretending you and I are engaged to be married is going to upset his plans.'

'I thought you might have guessed.' He came towards her, grasping her wrists and pulling her easily to her feet. 'My father, with his customary audacity, has decided yet again to choose a woman to warm my bed. But this time one of impeccable virtue—Irene Stavrolakes, the daughter of Manolis Stavrolakes, the shipping tycoon.' His harsh features were taut as his gaze lingered on Ginny's upraised face. 'It seems Pandelis is having a few tax problems with the Greek government and his burden would be greatly eased if he could form an association with Irene's father. Stavrolakes is willing to co-operate, but only if our two families are linked by marriage.'

'But what about Irene herself?' Amazed that anything so archaic could still exist, Ginny's astonished gaze searched his face for some sign that he was teasing her. 'Surely her father can't force her into a loveless marriage?'

'You find me so unattractive that you believe a woman would have to be forced to share my life and my bed?'

His expression held a note of mockery.

'*I* find your attitude far from captivating,' she returned spiritedly, 'and I don't believe any modern woman would agree to a marriage of convenience purely for dynastic reasons.' 'Unattractive' wasn't an adjective she would ever have applied to her irritating inquisitor—at least in the physical sense—but she wasn't about to feed his ego!

'That would depend on just how convenient she found it, surely? It wouldn't be the first time that two powerful families merged their business interests in the marriage bed.' His thumbs had found the palms of her hands and were circling leisurely against her warm skin, the slow, persistent movement disturbing her equilibrium. 'Irene is young and attractive and I have to admit for most men the bait would be extremely appetising.'

'But not for you?' she challenged coldly.

Steel's sable head dipped in agreement. 'I don't employ a broker to manage my affairs—business or personal.'

'Ugh...' A shudder accompanied Ginny's expression of disgust. 'It sounds so cold-blooded...' She was finding it difficult to meet the brooding intensity in Steel's luminous eyes, the close contact of his body causing her heart to beat too hurriedly for comfort.

'An adjective which could never be applied to me,' he purred softly. 'Which is just one of my father's misjudgements. The other one is in forgetting that I'm a lot older than I was the last time he procured a woman for me. I prefer to make my own arrangements now.'

CHAPTER SEVEN

A COLD, bright fire burned in Steel's narrowed eyes as the sweetness of anticipated revenge turned the corners of his beautiful mouth into a grimace.

'But why choose me?' Horrified to be cast into what appeared to be a Greek drama of frightening passions, Ginny swallowed hard, trying to hide her consternation. 'Surely there must be one *willing* woman in your life who'd oblige?'

'Oh, more than one, Ginny.' The quick assurance was accompanied by a humourless smile. 'Very willing and very difficult to jilt when her services were no longer required, and very expensive to pay off.' He paused, allowing his eyes to sweep over the soft curves of her breast outlined by the close-fitting material of her dress. Immediately she rued the impulse which had made her select it.

Clenching her teeth, she forced herself to bear his scrutiny without flinching, masking her mounting irritation as his eyes moved in steady speculation over her rigidly held form: from her tousled curls down the smooth lines of her dress, until they reached the elegant high-heeled sandals.

'But with you it's different,' he informed her softly, his inspection finished as his gaze rose to pin her own with unwavering intensity. 'Your co-operation comes free, because you're part of the package deal I've made with your father. The price of your compliance has already been paid. I owe you nothing, now or in the future. It's the perfect solution.'

'And my future doesn't matter? Do you suppose Howard will ever forgive me for this?' Ginny tugged her wrists, attempting to break Steel's hold, only to find it tightened.

'For your sake, I hope he doesn't,' he returned callously. 'Because by the time I've finished with you you'll be setting your sights a lot higher than a provincial schoolmaster, my lovely.' He released her hands and she stood there, rubbing her wrists, which had pinkened through her own unsuccessful struggles rather than by any overt brutality on Steel's part.

'I find your motives totally incomprehensible.' Scorn shone from her pale grey eyes and was echoed in the defiant lift of her chin. How dared he dismiss Howard so casually when he'd never met the man? 'Why can't you just refuse to marry Irene Stavrolakes and leave it at that?'

'Because it amuses me to produce a dark horse out of the hat.'

'That's a mixed metaphor.' Unable to reason with him, Ginny pounced on his lapse from perfect English, only to have her rebuke greeted with a flashing smile.

'You prefer I called you a rabbit? Ah, no, Ginny. You're no empty-headed fluffy bunny, more a headstrong filly who needs a steady hand on the bridle.' His pause was infinitesimal, accompanied by a lightning sweep of appraisal which traversed her curvaceous form, before he added softly, 'As well as some expert grooming before you enter the parade ring.'

'There's nothing wrong with the way I look!' She shifted indignantly from foot to foot. 'I don't have endless credit at Harrods!'

'You do now. A good hairstylist and couturier could transform you.' He pursed his mouth thoughtfully as her fists tightened in response to his impertinent survey. 'I don't think we need to bother with a crash course in deportment lessons—your carriage is excellent although a little stiff, and you have a natural grace of movement when you're not being deliberately obstreperous.'

'I also know the correct knives and forks to use at a formal dinner, eat asparagus with my fingers and break my bread roll instead of cutting it!' she flared back, infuriated beyond measure at his patronising tone. 'You may have a millionaire as a father but you don't have the prerogative on a good education or good manners!' She was seething with indignation, her eyes flashing a formidable challenge at Steel's cool countenance. 'I may have no option but to play your absurd game, but I'll do it my way. I won't be Eliza to your Professor Higgins, so you can keep your hairdressers and couturiers. You chose me—so you'll have to put up with me as I am!'

She was shaking with pent-up emotion as she stopped, oddly disturbed to see that her outburst hadn't achieved the result she'd intended. Instead of her defiance arousing Steel's wrath it seemed it had merely amused him.

'You may be right,' he concurred thoughtfully. 'Pandelis will be even more bemused and affronted if I produce a little waif with spiders' webs in her hair and a smut on her cheek as an alternative to the exquisite Irene. It should prove an entertaining meeting tomorrow, as well as providing a conversational gambit for the other guests.'

Panic swept through her. 'Tomorrow! You want me to meet your father so soon?' Deliberately ignoring his impertinent sarcasm, Ginny seized on this new intrusion into her privacy.

'But of course.' His gaze dwelt consideringly on her flushed cheeks. 'Naturally he expects to meet the woman he believes is about to become his daughter-in-law without delay. He faxed me at my London headquarters immediately the news reached him, and informed me that we're both expected to attend his name-day party at the Iliad hotel tomorrow evening.'

'So soon?' She caught her breath a little at his tone. 'I don't think I can put on a convincing act so soon. Can't you tell him it's not convenient?'

'When he's going to the trouble and expense to transfer the entire celebration from Athens to London at a moment's notice?' Steel's dark eyebrows reflected his astonishment. 'Don't worry, I'll ensure you're well-rehearsed. Having been taught by a master—or should I say mistress?—I can assure you I'm an excellent instructor.'

There was a twist to his sensuous mouth—a promising gleam in his dark eyes which threatened the core of Ginny's being as he closed the distance between them.

'Don't touch me!' She reared away from him, fear raising her tone a pitch as he ignored her order, gently taking her tense body and pulling it close against the unyielding strength of his own.

'Relax, *agape*.' The Greek endearment slipped from his mouth with the ease of familiarity. 'Lesson one— remember the other night at the Keys. You had no difficulty in relating to me then, did you?'

'No—because...'

He stopped her sentence in midstream by the simple recourse of sealing her lips with his own, stifling at birth the protestation she'd been about to repeat about missing Howard. She tried to fight him, but the battle was a mental one only as his kiss obliterated everything else, the predatory power of his body arousing alien and disturbing sensations, which disarmed her will-power.

Her head inclined back, she found herself clutching at Steel's shoulders, feeling the warmth of his skin burning through the thin fabric of his shirt, her heartbeat accelerating as she felt his fingers move caressingly down her back, following the line of her shoulder-blades, dropping to her waist, travelling to pursue the curve of her hips outlined by the smooth fabric of her dress.

Devastated by the avaricious assault of his mouth, she trembled in his embrace, her response instinctive, involuntary. For that moment she was enslaved by him, her thoughts fragmented as his hands and lips continued their hungry assault on her body, awakening a deep ache in the soft core of her body.

Shivers of delight were following the trailing fingers which caressed her, heat rippling in waves in the path of the sensuous massage. Her breasts, crushed against the hardness of his chest, seemed to have acquired a sensitivity she had never experienced before, the apices pulsating with a life of their own, hardening and thrusting achingly against the restraining wall of Steel's chest.

She moved her own gentle hands down the corded muscles of his arms, feeling the power of the tension which armed his superb male body, amazed and a little scared because in all their time together Howard had never touched her with such controlled power, such aching intensity.

Steel's lips left hers to trail their soft persuasiveness across her cheek, then he was whispering something incomprehensible in her ear, releasing her from his arms, taking her hands from his own shoulders, holding them for a brief moment before letting them fall back to hang trembling at her sides.

For a moment she was stunned, dazed by her own response, then as her senses returned she began to shake with shame and regret, furious with herself that she should have lost her self-control, betrayed her vulnerability to a man who was callously indifferent towards her as a person.

Painful heat flooding her cheeks, she turned her head, managing to avoid his gaze while she fought the tumultuous sensations his actions had conjured up inside her. Then her pride came to her aid.

'There's no call to behave like an animal!' she cried, anger scalding her throat, hot and violent enough to quench the tears of humiliation which had threatened to betray her.

'But I am an animal, Ginny.' His soft laugh was doubly disconcerting. 'A male animal with all that implies—and a true son of my father.'

'Is that some kind of threat?' she demanded.

His smile encompassed her, sending a small shiver of trepidation through her nervous system.

'I don't need threats where you're concerned, do I, Ginny?' he asked, continuing to speak without giving her a chance to answer. 'You asked for coaching and I supplied it. And it's pointless for you to play the outraged virgin, because we both know that you're neither. From the moment I walked into Leo's office, there were sparks flying between us.'

Ignoring her quick gasp of denial, he added coolly, 'Why else would I have asked you out to dinner? And why did you accept? You must have realised I already had ample brochures.'

'There was certainly friction between us!' She was so furious at his patronising confession, she could hardly bring herself to stay civil. All that time he'd wasted asking her questions to which he already knew the answers! 'But that was because you were ill-mannered and abusive——'

'If that's what you prefer to believe.' He shrugged off her protest with a disbelieving smile. 'But if I hadn't been sure of your co-operation I wouldn't have lied to Leo. So let's have an end to this nonsense, shall we? Phone Howard and tell him he's a free man, before he reads it in the papers for himself and takes umbrage.'

'I'll do it tomorrow,' she croaked. Her mouth felt dry and she wanted to scream out a denial of everything Steel had said, but her larynx seemed frozen. 'I'm too tired now, and he's probably out at the opera—or something.'

'Or something,' Steel agreed silkily. 'Do I take it you intend to retire for the night already?'

'With your permission,' she returned sarcastically. 'I've made up the spare room for you—first right at the top of the stairs—but I expect you've already discovered that for yourself.'

'Leo invited me to make myself at home,' he agreed cheerfully. 'But your duties for the night aren't quite complete yet, I'm afraid, *agape mou*.'

On her way to the door, Ginny was halted in her tracks, Steel's earlier attestation to their mutual physical attraction still ringing in her ears.

Unsuccessfully attempting to still the tremor of apprehension which was flowing like an icy stream through her veins, she forced herself to meet the mocking laughter which lurked at the back of his eyes. 'Let's get one thing perfectly straight,' she said. 'I've agreed to partner you in this game you're hell-bent on playing because my father's peace of mind is at stake. I'll meet Pandelis and I'll act as your housekeeper if that's what you want, until you decide you've had enough fun at his expense. But whatever other duties you envisage don't and won't include my sharing my bed with anyone!'

'Have it your own way.' Steel's wide shoulders moved in a negligible shrug. 'Actually it was food I was thinking about rather than sleeping quarters.'

'But you've been fed.' Amazed, she looked down at his empty plate and the crumpled napkin. 'I thought you'd had enough——'

'Not me, Ginny,' he said gently. 'Kefi. His needs are greater than mine at the moment.'

Mortified at her misunderstanding, with her head held high she marched towards the kitchen. How could she have allowed her equilibrium to be so disturbed that she'd forgotten the duties she owed the kitten to which she'd opened her heart and her home?

But when she entered the room, Kefi was curled up in the basket Steel had provided for him, fast asleep, leaving her in no doubt that he'd been adequately fed and watered. So Steel's admonition had been deliberately provocative, intended to unsettle her, keep her on her toes. An attitude which didn't promise well for her short-term future as his bride-to-be!

* * *

It was six o'clock the following morning when she staggered downstairs to make herself some toast and coffee and give Kefi his breakfast before letting him out into the large garden at the back of the house, knowing that the promise of regular meals would ensure his safe return at regular intervals.

The forecast promised no change in the warm, sunny weather, and even at that early hour the atmosphere was still and promising, sweetened by birdsong and the perfume of roses. Determined not to make a similar mistake to yesterday's, when her dress had attracted such unwanted and unwarranted attention from her aggravating house guest, she'd dressed in jeans and a demure shirt, the sleeves rolled up workman-like above her elbows.

How could she have been so unprepared for the unwelcome effects of Steel's 'lesson'? she chided herself, staring morosely at the dark liquid in her mug, inhaling its fragrance. That first ruthless kiss in the Keys should have armed her self-preservation alarm bells; and how ironical it was that her father's concern about suburban crime had placed her in a situation more threatening to her peace of mind than any anxiety she felt about the possibility of alien danger lurking in the quiet avenues of Surrey!

Exhaling in a deep sigh, she sipped the coffee, acknowledging that for the first time in her life her body was refusing to conform to the strictures of her mind. It was an unnerving experience. A wry smile turned the corners of her mouth, as she brushed a wayward tendril of tawny hair away from her cheek. Perhaps learning how to deal with the first mutinous surge of previously controlled hormones was like learning to drive a car, she surmised with mocking insight: harder to do as one got older.

Replacing the mug on the table, she stared down at the diamond and sapphire cluster ring which graced her finger. An expensive symbol of a meaningless and mercenary arrangement. Steel had made his attitude towards women very plain. He was the hunter and they the willing prey. But not she—not Ginette Sullivan!

She nibbled at a slice of toast, delaying the moment when she'd have to phone Rome. It wasn't the way she'd have chosen to tell Howard about her supposed liaison. She might have realised she didn't love him, but he deserved something better than a phone call to inform him of the fact; but Steel was right. He had to be put in the picture without delay, for everyone's sake.

As a slight sound above her head distracted her, she sprang to her feet, her lips compressed. Despite her qualms, the sooner she spoke to Howard the better! The last thing she needed was Steel Anastasi eavesdropping on a conversation which she sensed was going to be both painful and humiliating to both parties.

It took only a few moments before she was on her way to the phone, the holiday brochure with the hotel's number grasped in her hand. In common with the office, Leo Sullivan hadn't felt the need to modernise the interior of his house, so the only telephone was in the hall. Grateful that there was no sign of her uninvited guest, Ginny dialled the international number, a spurt of anxiety quickening her pulse as she asked to be connected to Howard Sinclair.

An unexpected shiver convulsed her as she waited. Possibly caused by the coolness of the hall after the warmth of the sunny dining-room, or more probably by apprehension of the task ahead of her, she realised shakily as she waited for the familiar sound of Howard's voice.

'Hello—yes?'

Ginny jumped nervously as clear tones sounded distinctly in her ear, the accent English, the register feminine.

'I'm sorry, I must have been put through to the wrong room. I asked to speak to Howard Sinclair.' Her fingers tightened around the receiver in frustration. 'Can you——?'

'Who the hell is it? Not that idiot in Room Service again?'

She gasped as Howard's unmistakable voice, irritable and gruff, sounded in her ear.

'Here, give me the phone, Coralie, I'll sort him out!'

Momentarily stunned, Ginny stood rigid, clutching the receiver, unable to utter a word as her ears picked up the sound of movement at the other end of the line, followed by Howard's voice even louder in her ear. 'Look here—we want exactly the same as we had yesterday morning. It's quite simple to understand...'

'It certainly is, Howard.' Her power of speech returned and with it an unexpected sense of humour. 'Even for someone as dumb as I am.'

'Ginny? Is that you, Ginny?'

'That's right,' she confirmed mildly, astonished at how well she was controlling her voice now she'd regained its use. Stilling the desire to laugh at the horror which had lifted Howard's own pleasant timbre a couple of tones, she continued pleasantly, 'You can't imagine how pleased I am to find out you're having a good time without me.'

'Listen, Ginny—it's not what it seems——'

'Of course it is.' Calmly she interrupted his spluttered protestations, feeling a terrible weight of guilt beginning to lighten as she acknowledged that Steel's cynical prognosis of Howard's activities had proved uncannily correct. 'We both know it's exactly what it seems, so please don't waste time denying it.'

The ensuing silence at the other end of the line wiped out any last vestige of doubt she might have harboured about there being an innocent explanation for Howard and Coralie being about to enjoy a breakfast *à deux*, and she continued evenly, 'I think even before we planned to go to Rome together, Howard, you and I were both beginning to suspect there wasn't going to be a long-term future together for us, weren't we?'

'Damn it, Ginny! You're hardly in a position to condemn me!' Embarrassment changed to hostility as Howard sprang to his own defence. 'You were never very free with your favours, were you? In fact frigid is the word which springs to mind. When you agreed we should go on holiday together I hoped you'd grown up a little, finally shaken off your father's Victorian influence. I can understand why you're upset, but these things happen——'

'Of course they do, Howard.' Stung by his references to her father and the blistering pain of the label he'd pinned on her reluctance to indulge in casual sex, she interrupted his blustering. To her relief, telling him about Steel was becoming easier by the moment. 'And not only to men,' she countered evenly. 'In fact, that's why I'm ringing you.' She took a deep breath because her hand which was holding the receiver had begun to tremble. 'I've met someone else, too, Howard. I wanted you to be one of the first to know.'

There, it was done. There was a moment's tense silence, during which she felt a wave of nausea sweep through her. Tarnished dreams maybe, but they'd been all she'd had. Now she had nothing.

'I see.' There was a whispering at the other end of the line, before Howard's voice sounded once more in her ear. 'Look, Ginny, you're not just saying that, are you, to get your own back? I mean, you really have met someone else?' he asked cautiously.

'His name's Steel Anastasi.' A great bubble of released tension broke in her chest, as intoxicating as yesterday's champagne, heady, exhilarating and totally unexpected. She'd spent all night dreading this moment, believing Howard would be angry and belligerent. Instead, after his initial stunned reaction, he seemed to be bearing up remarkably well.

Steel had been right when he'd opined that the interests of both her father and herself were among Howard's lowest priorities. She could see it clearly now. As clearly as her own reflection in the hall mirror. Howard had never loved her, not in the way she needed to be loved.

'Ginny...are you still there?' Howard's voice, more restrained now, impinged on her thoughts.

'Uh-huh.' She made a small sound of acquiescence.

'Coralie's just gone into the bathroom, so I can speak frankly. I met her in the Piazza Navona the night I arrived. She was with a group of students—all very friendly.' He sounded embarrassed.

'I can imagine,' Ginny allowed generously, envisaging his fair complexion colouring at the admission. She could even feel sympathy at his obvious uneasiness at the way his orderly life must have been disrupted by the winsome and willing Coralie.

'But you're right, Ginny.' His tone had regained its normal slightly pedantic nature. 'It wasn't really working out for us, you and me, not as a couple contemplating marriage, and when you chose to stay in Taychapel, rather than go ahead with the holiday we'd planned, well...'

'You realised that you didn't want to marry me after all?' she enquired brightly, biting back the retort that, as he was perfectly aware, she'd given up her holiday not through any desire to thwart or inconvenience him, or to deny him the sexual fulfilment he considered his right, but because her father might die.

'I realised you had other priorities in your life,' he amended, a hint of familiar pomposity sharpening his tone. 'The wife of a headmaster needs to show commitment to her husband, and you were well aware of my ambitions.'

'Of course, you're quite right, Howard,' she said meekly, allowing him his moment of superiority. 'I'm glad you're not upset. It was never my intention to cause you embarrassment or distress you in any way.'

'On the contrary, Ginny. I'm glad you've reached the same conclusion as I have. I wasn't looking forward to telling you I'd had second thoughts about continuing our relationship—although *I* would have waited until I was back in England to tell you to your face.'

She swallowed the implicit rebuke, knowing it was merited. 'I didn't want to do it this way either,' she admitted honestly, 'but Steel insisted it was your right to be told immediately.'

'Well, I hope for your sake you aren't making a big mistake.' Howard's tone was heavily patronising. 'For God's sake, Ginny, how well do you know this man? Have you considered he might be a fortune-hunter?'

'No, actually.' She stifled the laughter which welled in her throat at the uncomplimentary question. With a struggle she resisted the temptation to inform Howard that Steel's father was a millionaire. Not only did it seem a petty point to score, but she doubted if Howard would believe it. He would certainly not believe the truth. No sane person would!

Over the phone came the sound of a door opening, followed by a soft giggle, before Howard spoke again, his voice warmer and more relaxed. 'Look, Ginny, I have to go now. Is there anything else?'

The insensitive question fired a spark of spirit in her heart. 'Just that I'm sure you'll be pleased to hear that my father is progressing very well after his operation, and that he totally approves of Steel.'

The sudden sound of footsteps on the landing overhead gave her just the excuse she needed to terminate the conversation. 'I'll have to go now. Steel's just got up and will be wanting his breakfast. I'm so happy that we've got matters straightened out between us without any acrimony, and I hope we can still be friends,' she said graciously. Not pausing as she heard his mumbled agreement to her sincere but trite wish, she went on, 'Enjoy the rest of your holiday, Howard—and give my love to Coralie.'

CHAPTER EIGHT

IT WAS only when Ginny replaced the receiver gently on its rest that she became aware of the increased rhythm of her heart as it responded to the surge of adrenalin which had sustained her. Leaning against the wall, eyes closed, she breathed deeply. Where was the depression, the sadness at the end of an era? she wondered in amazement. Far from the feelings of guilt and unhappiness she'd anticipated, she was filled with a sense of freedom, like a kite that had wrenched its string from the hand of its manipulator, free at last to soar on a heady voyage of discovery.

'So, how did he take the news?'

Abruptly her eyes flared open. Steel stood before her, freshly shaven but barefooted, a silk robe covering his body from neck to knees, displaying a V of light brown skin between the lapels and, beneath the hem of the garment, calves of a similar colour, their shapely outline furred by a light covering of soft dark hair.

'He was devastated, of course!' she snapped, prevaricating to save face. No way was she going to let this arrogant Greek guess that Howard's future plans had apparently long ceased to include her. 'Is that why you've got up at the crack of dawn—to check I obeyed your instructions?'

Following the direction of his interested gaze, she realised crossly that one button too many on her shirt had burst open to reveal a cleavage she'd supposed covered. Hastily she made efforts to repair the damage.

'One of the reasons,' he agreed calmly, 'but there were others and, for your information, dawn broke a long time ago.'

'So did my heart,' she lied coldly.

'Really?' He didn't seem impressed. 'You don't appear to be greatly distressed.'

Dropping her eyes from his too encompassing gaze, Ginny felt a sudden urgency to put distance between them. She sensed danger in his mood, as if he was a predator already alerted to the scent of his prey, and she was neither physically nor emotionally adequately prepared to deal with it.

'Since Howard will never forgive me for what he sees as a betrayal, or the manner in which I was forced to deliver it, it's something I've got to live with, isn't it?' She tossed him a savage glare before staring disparagingly at his informal attire. 'Now you've satisfied yourself I've complied with your orders, I assume you'll be wanting to go upstairs and get dressed?'

He flashed her a smile which did strange things to her equilibrium. 'You find my bare feet offensive? You prefer me to wear socks, perhaps?'

'Don't you have any shoes?' she demanded imperiously, certain that he was perfectly aware that it wasn't the bare skin she could see that worried her, but rather the suspicion that the short robe covered a great deal more unclothed flesh.

'Strange.' He regarded her musingly. 'My girlfriends have always told me how ridiculous they find men who prance around naked except for their socks or shoes, but if that's what you prefer...'

'Who said anything about naked?' She cast him a distasteful look. He must have picked up her unsettling suspicion about his lack of underclothing, and was amusing himself by playing on her susceptibilities.

'In view of the fact that ours is a business arrangement, I expect to be treated with more consideration than a—a...'

'A what, Ginny?' The enquiry sounded disarmingly mild, but it was belied by the sudden glint in the dark eyes which challenged her to find an acceptable word for the stream of women which must have flowed through his life.

'A passing fancy.' She felt a surge of relief as her vocabulary suggested a phrase which would illustrate her feelings without being too dangerously insulting to Steel's predilections towards female company. 'And I'd prefer you to come down to breakfast fully dressed.'

'Really?' His eyebrows lifted as he managed to make the word sound as if she'd suggested something lewd. 'I promise I'll give the matter some thought for the future. In the meantime I can assure you I'm wearing more clothes than I would do on the beach. Now, how about a cup of coffee?'

'All right.' She shrugged, ignoring the invitation to oppose him further. 'Where would you like it?'

'Preferably not in my lap, *agape mou*.' Obviously she hadn't been as successful in concealing her irritation as she'd hoped. 'It could cause a disablement I would have great difficulty in explaining away to Pandelis. The living-room will suit me fine.'

He walked away with a smirk, whistling softly between his beautiful white teeth.

So this was going to be the pattern of the immediate future, was it? Forbidden to occupy herself in the office, accountable for all her actions, she'd been allocated the role of complaisant housekeeper. And *'agape mou'*? Huh! Clearly that was an endearment she would have to learn to live with in the coming days.

He was standing gazing out of the window as she entered the living-room, a breakfast mug of coffee clutched in her hand. She'd turned the power off from under the percolator, so even if she had been unable to resist the temptation to throw it at him he would have been drenched rather than disfigured, but she managed to hand it over with quiet dignity.

'Thanks.' He took it from her, onyx eyes scrutinising the taut lines of her pretty face. 'Still no tears for lost love?' Lifting the mug to his lips, he continued to watch her over the rim as he began to drink.

She shot him a withering glance. 'What good are tears? The damage is already done. All the tears in the world won't repair it.'

'Some things are better left broken, Ginny.'

He continued to eye her lazily as he finished the coffee in a long draught before placing the mug on a nearby table.

'If you say so,' she agreed coolly, winging a silent prayer of thanks to heaven that he had no idea of Howard's self-indulgence in Rome, or how her erstwhile fiancé had already decided she wasn't suitable to be his wife. 'I'll get you another coffee.'

Anxious to escape his disturbing presence, she moved quickly, reaching for the empty mug, only to be restrained by a gentle hand on her upper arm as Steel frustrated her action.

'Good, then we're in total agreement,' he said softly, his compelling eyes riveting her to the spot.

His nearness was overwhelming, the warmth of his palm penetrating the thin cotton of her blouse, the controlled power of his fingers forming a light but formidable cage as they halted her progress. Raising her chin defiantly, Ginny forced herself to meet the unblinking regard of his dark stare, silently cursing the overprotectiveness which had made her father insist on this—this playboy being cast in the role of bodyguard.

With wary eyes she evaluated the lean thrust of his jaw, the hard-boned beauty of what she thought of as a very Greek face with its strongly sculpted lines and outstanding attraction of dark, heavily lashed eyes.

'Relax, *agape mou.*' His eyes lingered on the unsteady curve of her mouth. 'You've done very well.' He raised his free hand, trailing one lean finger to trace the outlines of her querulous lips. 'You really do have a lovely face,' he mused as if to himself. 'I have a feeling I'm going to find more than one compensation in this business arrangement of ours.'

'Not if you're expecting me to provide it!' Leaping to her own defence, Ginny tried to ignore the strange effect that the warmth of Steel's mocking smile was having on her pulse-rate.

'Is that a challenge?'

The softness of his voice was more threatening than if he'd raised it in anger. Mutely Ginny moved her head, not caring for its silky note, but she'd left it too late to escape as his arresting hand slid quickly from her captured arm to encompass her waist, easing her towards his own body, pinning her against him.

'More like a forecast.' His gaze raked over her up-turned face. 'The other night when I took you out to dinner and you turned your charming nose up at everything about me, I promised myself I'd make you change your mind.'

'It was just a bit of fun!' Ginny tried to feign a careless laugh, but it died in her throat as his eyes locked with hers for a long moment and she felt a cold sweat begin to break out all over her.

'I wasn't amused.'

'But—but...' She shook her head, unable to think straight because the casual caress of his spatulate fingers against the small of her back was doing odd things to her mental processes as well as sending a strange warmth speeding through her veins, to replace the previous chill which had assailed her.

Her muscles deprived of power, she found herself unable to resist as Steel lowered his head. She wanted to oppose him, but as his purposeful lips touched hers her defences crumbled and she found herself yielding beneath the persuasive, erotic incursion of his tongue into her soft, vulnerable mouth.

Uttering a cry, half-protest, half-pleasure, she labored to find coherence as his fingers moved to caress her firm, full breasts, only to find her voice muted by the continuing hungry salutation of his mouth as it touched her own with liquid fire.

Vibrantly alive to the hard masculinity of his body, her senses began to respond joyously to him—the scent of his skin, the exciting, intoxicating taste of him, the tantalising pressure of his mouth, paradoxically both hard and soft at the same time.

'Ah, Ginny, you're like ambrosia and nectar.' Steel swept her seemingly boneless body off its feet, lifting her in his arms, whispering against the skin of her throat as he turned with her to lower her on to the couch. 'And you're warm and soft and trembling like an aspen in my arms...'

She was sinking into the soft cushions, entranced by the husky depths of his voice, the passion-glazed luminosity of his half-shuttered eyes as he leaned across her.

Lost in a time warp, she trembled with mindless expectation as his hand closed once more on the thrusting curve of her breast with a sensitive caress. His fingers slid within the neck of her shirt, to compel a whimper of pleasure from her which was drowned by his exclamation of delight as the tumid bud responded to his touch.

'Steel...' His name was a lingering caress on her tongue as blindly she acknowledged the need he was evoking. Sliding her hands up his silk-covered back, she felt with a thrill of joy the tuned masculine muscles respond to their massage; heard his steady indrawn breath; felt his ardent body quieten above her although the heavy bombardment of his heart continued to speak to her own through the thin pieces of cloth which kept their eloquent flesh apart.

Then he was rolling away from her, running his fingers through his tumbled hair, getting to his feet and stalking to the other side of the room.

Engulfed by a wave of shame, Ginny struggled upright, her fingers scrabbling to rebutton her shirt. She should be outraged at the liberties he had taken; instead she'd been a willing partner to her own humiliation. Shamefully, far from resenting his actions, her resentment had only blossomed the moment he had halted them!

'A worthy performance, Ginny! I congratulate you.' Steel spun round on his heel, tightening the sash of his robe, to regard her with a faintly supercilious smile. 'A bystander could easily have been fooled into believing that you really enjoyed the experience.'

One glance at his face and she saw that he'd regained his poise far quicker than she, only the slight flush across his hard cheekbones betraying that he hadn't been entirely unaffected by her mindless response.

Pulse thumping, every nerve taut, Ginny faced him without flinching, desperate to regain a smidgen of self-respect. 'Or realise, perhaps, how practised a gigolo you are!' She heaved in a painful breath born of mortification and the need to defend herself. 'After all, you did have professional training, didn't you?'

The words were out before she could stop them. Instantly appalled that she'd sunk to taunting him with the memory of Louli's betrayal, she raised her hand to her mouth as if to obliterate the words.

'True.' The single syllable was like the flick of a whip. 'And if I hadn't changed my mind at the last moment you would have succumbed to my expertise, would you not, *agape mou*?'

'Is that part of the bargain, Steel?' She couldn't deny it as shame brought the blood surging to her face. 'Am I to be part of the fringe benefits you hope to enjoy when the partnership agreement between you and my father is finally signed?'

'An interesting proposition.' His lips twisted, a flash of sarcasm illuminating the depth of his sable eyes as they dwelt on her flushed face. 'But I can assure you there's nothing in the small print which gives me the right to enjoy your highly delightful but hardly unique body.' He paused, then laughed softly at her rebelliously tilted chin, his voice silky yet oddly menacing as it caressed her ears. 'Believe me, the day you wake up and find yourself in my bed will be the day you admit that you came there willingly, not because you were coerced, but because it was where you wanted to be.'

Never! Uncontrollable panic rose in Ginny's chest as a wave of apprehension swept through her. Inhaling a deep breath, she tried to regain control of her emotions, averting her eyes to stare at the carpet, unable to meet the bland half-smile which had twisted Steel's mouth. His impatient sigh penetrated her discomfort.

'And now we've established what I *don't* want from you, perhaps you'll listen while I tell you exactly what I *do* require!'

'Please do.' Somehow she managed to keep her voice expressionless, and her hands from seeking to repair the ravages he'd made to her hair and her body as, forcing her knees together to stop their trembling, she clenched her fists in her lap.

'I have a lot of work to do today.' His attitude was businesslike as he tightened the belt which held the edges of his robe together and began to spell out his programme with military precision. Any less physically imposing a man would have looked ridiculous, Ginny thought as her concentration wavered, but Steel managed to look like a cross between Alexander the Great and Mark Antony. A formidable and frightening combination. Alexander was reputed to have conquered half the known world by the time he was thirty, and as for Mark Antony—well, everyone who'd read Shakespeare knew the havoc he'd wreaked in the heart of the Egyptian Queen Cleopatra! How many conquests had Steel Anastasi notched up during his thirty-two years on the planet? she wondered hazily.

'Ginny, are you listening?'

The sound of her name on his lips seized her attention.

'Of course,' she lied quickly. 'You were talking about the work you have to do today.'

The impatient breath he heaved acknowledged that her inattention had not escaped his notice. 'I was telling you I've already briefed a barrister to appeal against the enforcement order. He's an excellent man, the best in his field and, having seen the full documentation, doesn't anticipate any problems in getting the original decision finally and irrevocably overturned. Also I expect the formal agreement giving me a full mandate to act for Sullivan's in Leo's absence to be ready by tomorrow at the latest.'

Impressed despite herself, Ginny nodded. Thrumming like an overworked dynamo, Steel's powerful personality seemed to dominate the room, robbing her of the power of speech.

'I've left full instructions with Duncan and Cathy as to the work I need done in the office,' he continued, ticking off the points on the fingers of one of his capable hands. Ginny shuddered, recalling just how capable those hands had been in arousing feelings inside her she'd never suspected she possessed. With an effort she compelled her attention to concentrate on business as his deep-timbred voice went on, 'And I've called for a complete overhaul of stock. That should keep the rest of the staff busy.

'I've also arranged for a computer system to be installed. There are excellent business software packages available but I want certain adaptations made to tailor the output to Sullivan's specific requirements. My intention is to employ two school-leavers with good A levels in computing to learn the new system from scratch——'

'You're going to get rid of Duncan!' She sprang to her feet, horrified at the implication of his words. 'Duncan's been with Sullivan's since Dad took over from Grandpa!'

'My dear girl, Duncan is already sixty-three,' he retorted briskly. 'In any case he wouldn't be leaving immediately because we'll have to run the two systems, computer and manual, in tandem for some time until we're satisfied everything is working well.'

'Dad will never allow it!' Ginny's features contorted with shock and anger as she confronted him boldly. 'He'll let Duncan go on working just as long as he wants to!'

'And have you asked him how long that is?' he demanded harshly, continuing without giving her a chance to reply. 'No, of course you haven't. Because you've never been here long enough to find out anything about the business, or its employees. Well, take my word for it—Duncan is counting the days to his retirement. He can't wait to go and live next door to his married daughter on the coast so he can see his grandchildren regularly. The only reason he hasn't taken early retirement is because up until now Sullivan's could neither spare him nor make it financially viable for him to do so.'

Steel was angry, whether with her or because Sullivan's was in a far worse state than he'd at first suspected Ginny couldn't say; but she felt his annoyance seep into every pore of her skin, chilling her blood. How reasonable his explanation sounded—but she didn't trust him. Couldn't trust him. Not after the way he'd just disturbed her equilibrium with such careless skill.

'And Cathy?' she countered, keeping her voice level with an effort. 'I suppose you're going to let Cathy go too?'

Wide shoulders moved beneath the silken covering which disguised their strength. 'She has plans to marry.'

'Cathy? Marry? But she's a grandmother!' Astonishment raised her normal mellow tones a full pitch.

'She's also a woman and a widow,' Steel rejoined crisply. 'You believe that the so-called joys of marriage should be reserved for the young and beautiful?'

'No, of course not!' Ginny swallowed miserably. 'It's just that she's such an efficient secretary—well, assistant really, and that Dad and she get on so well together. He relies on her,' she protested, her heart sinking as Steel's face remained adamant. 'He'll be lost without her.' A thought occurred to her. 'Perhaps I could take her place?' she offered tentatively. 'I don't have secretarial skills but I am reasonably conversant with computers and word processors, and I'm a quick learner——'

'No.' The brief interjection stopped her in her tracks. 'The time when you might have served a useful purpose at Sullivan's, other than lending a decorative presence, has long passed. The days of amateurism here are over, Ginny. The professionals have taken over.' The insolence in his voice was ill-concealed. 'The sooner you come to terms with that fact, the happier you'll be.'

Inside she was fuming, but an inner caution warned her she had nothing to gain either personally or professionally by engaging in a war of attrition with her father's condescending partner.

'Fine with me.' She rose to her feet, standing facing him, hands splayed on her hips, the soft palms aware of the rub of tough denim beneath them. 'So now I know all the jobs I'm precluded from doing, may I ask what plans you *do* have for me today?'

'Nothing too onerous, *agape mou*.' The belligerence of her stance seemed to amuse him, and there was a spark of some indefinable emotion in the depth of the dark eyes which smiled at her. 'I thought you might like to make me some toast while I get dressed. Afterwards, you may do as you please with two provisos, the first being that it has nothing to do with the day-to-day running of Sullivan's and the second that you're suitably dressed and ready to leave for Pandelis's party by eight o'clock tonight.'

'To hear is to obey, o mighty one!' Biting back her irritation at his patronising manner, Ginny took refuge in sarcasm, sweeping him a derisory bow. 'Does the master require sustenance at lunchtime or before leaving for the party?' she enquired, opening her grey eyes to their fullest width, assuming an expression of utter guilelessness.

'Be sure that if he does the mistress will be the first to know!' He sauntered away from her with a power and feline grace that Kefi would have found hard to match as Ginny bit her lip in chagrin, furious with herself that she'd offered him the opportunity for the *double entendre*, and unable to think fast enough to counter its suggestiveness.

At the door he turned. 'Oh, and Ginny, do you have any honey? Preferably Greek from the slopes of Mount Parnassus? I have a sudden fancy for the taste of home.' Not waiting for her answer, he strode lissomly across the threshold, his bare feet padding noiselessly on the thick carpet as he made his way back upstairs, humming softly a tune which seemed strangely familiar, but to which she could put no name.

It was only when she'd set the bread in the toaster and discovered a jar of honey, smugly pleased to discover it was from good English clover-fed bees, that she realised where she'd heard the melody before: in the Keys of Corfu, when she'd sobbed out her despair in Steel's arms and he had consoled her with that breathless, open-mouthed, passionate kiss which had prefaced her present misfortune.

She breathed a sigh of relief when Steel eventually left the house. He'd even robbed her of her planned display of mock-despair at not having been able to provide the honey of his choice by the simple means of not commenting on it at all, she realised wryly as she set about a few household tasks.

Entering the spare room, she was surprised to see that Steel had made his own bed. Somehow she'd supposed he would have left that task to her, but no. The room was as tidy and clean is it had been when he'd moved in.

Scooping up Kefi, who had followed her upstairs, she spent half an hour playing with him in the garden, before deciding to water the runner beans and tomatoes which her father was growing. By the time she'd finished the hospital would be open for visitors and that was where she planned to spend the rest of the morning.

As soon as she entered her father's room an hour or so later and saw the improvement in his appearance, her heart began to sing.

'The doctor's very pleased with me,' he confirmed. 'A few more days and I should be on solid food again. It won't be long now, darling, before I'll be home.' His voice had a new strength and optimism, but beneath the surge of joy she felt at the obvious signs of his recovery Ginny's heart gave a painful lurch. How much of his future plans had Steel imparted?

Uncertain whether or not she should even hint that there might be changes ahead, Ginny's troubled eyes fastened on Leo's smiling gaze as he continued blithely, 'My future son-in-law has great plans for the business, you know, Ginny. Really means to put it on the map. Give it the thrust into the next century that it needs, but which I could never have found the capital to provide.' He shook his head reprovingly at her, but his smile deepened. 'To think I was worried about you—afraid that you really would go ahead and marry Howard and relegate yourself to being nothing but an appendage to his ambition—the headmaster's wife—the mother of the headmaster's children...'

'You disliked him that much, Dad?' she asked, bewildered. 'I knew you didn't get on brilliantly——'

'I didn't actively dislike him, Ginny.' Leo reached out and took her hand. 'I just didn't think he was good enough for my daughter. But since that's what most fathers think anyway, I kept my mouth shut.'

'But you do approve of Steel?' she asked, thinking how ironic the question was.

Leo nodded. 'He's a man of integrity, Ginny. I've been doing business with him long enough to realise that.' Amusement shone in his eyes. 'He can also keep his own counsel—as you of all people must be aware!'

For a moment Ginny was puzzled, then enlightenment dawned. 'Oh, you mean not telling you until now that we knew each other,' she said awkwardly, wondering how she was going to talk her way out of that one!

'It's all right, love,' Leo hastened to reassure her. 'Of course I understand your motives. Steel's already explained that he didn't feel free to tell me at the time that he was seeing you in Birmingham, because you hadn't fully made your mind up about Howard's place in your life. Then, of course, you were waiting until he was back in England so you could tell me the news together, and I delayed your plans further by getting ill.' He chuckled. 'If I hadn't turned down his offer of financial help and explained why, I dare say I still wouldn't know you were in love with each other.'

'Probably.' Ginny gave him a wan smile as he squeezed her hand.

'Truly, it was the best tonic you could have given me! Even my specialist is surprised at the speed of my recovery.'

'Well, you don't need to hire the church hall yet, Dad.' A stab of guilt pricked Ginny's heart as she envisaged the disappointment in store for him when Steel had finished amusing himself at her expense and she returned his ring. 'We haven't exactly named the day.'

Leo's answering smile betrayed the deep happiness of a man whose vision of the future comprised dreams fulfilled, and filled her heart with a great emptiness. 'Knowing Steel as well as I do, darling, I guarantee you'll be a bride before winter,' he told her confidently.

CHAPTER NINE

IT WAS two hours later before Ginny left the hospital. Talk about skating on thin ice, she thought grimly, easing the Renault into the mainstream traffic. For a girl about to be married, her knowledge of her future husband's background and lifestyle was pitiful. Thankfully, her father appeared to have sensed nothing adverse in her reticence, and had chatted quite comfortably about his own liking for the other man. From everything he'd said it was obvious that there was a real rapport between the two men. Heaven have pity on Leo Sullivan when that trust was shattered, she prayed earnestly.

Arriving back at the yard in the late afternoon, she was astonished to find a large container lorry blocking her access. The badly delayed but very welcome cargo which had been blockaded on the Continent had arrived at last and without warning!

The scene was one of mild chaos as Sam, the delivery man, struggled to unload and stack a large number of cartons on a forklift truck, while Cathy and Duncan struggled to manhandle the smaller cartons.

It was just what she needed. With so much unexpended energy surging through her system, and only too glad for the opportunity to engage in some physical labour, it took Ginny only minutes to park the Renault and join the fray.

It was six o'clock before the last carton had been checked and safely stored and everyone had departed, leaving her in sole occupation of the yard and office. Flushed with effort, glowing with the satisfaction of a job well done and considerably dirtier than when she'd started, Ginny made her way to the office, sinking down on one of the chairs, but not before she'd helped herself to one of Cathy's cans of orangeade kept in the cupboard for such emergencies. Pulling the tab, she quenched her thirst, tipping her head back, too weary to find a cup, swallowing the contents direct from the can, closing her eyes in ecstasy as the comparatively cool liquid refreshed her parched throat.

'I thought I might find you here.' The slightly menacing tone in Steel's pleasantly modulated voice brought Ginny's eyes open with a start as her head rocketed forward in shock.

'Well, someone had to help Sam,' she retorted defensively, eyeing his dark grey business suit disapprovingly. 'The European shipment's been delivered and if I hadn't been available you'd have crates lying all over the yard instead of being properly stacked and locked away for the night.'

Steel's lips compressed briefly, then relaxed as his eyes took in her appearance. '"A sweet disorder in the dress" suits you, Ginny. I find your flushed cheeks, dirty face and tousled hair quite charming and your unbuttoned shirt enchanting. So enchanting in fact that I forgive you for disobeying my orders.'

'Am I supposed to be grateful for such a gracious pardon?' she flashed back angrily, fingers already attempting to redress the state of her shirt, irritated even further to discover that one button had disappeared completely. Reaching to a tin on the desk, she found and

jabbed a pin into the offending material, conscious that
Steel was regarding her efforts with an amused smile.

'On the contrary, it's I who should feel gratitude,
agape mou.' He laughed softly at the rebellious tone of
her voice. 'If you hadn't come to the rescue, I would
have been obliged to do the job myself, which would
have delayed our plans for the evening.'

'Oh—the party...' Unbelievable though it seemed,
during the past hectic hours the prospect of the ordeal
she'd been dreading had been completely eradicated from
her mind. Desperately conscious of the aching muscles
of her arms and back, even the protest of her thigh
muscles due to reaching and stretching, Ginny's
weariness increased. 'I can't possibly go out tonight; I'm
exhausted. You'll have to make my excuses—say I'm not
well.'

'But that would be a lie.' The air between them suddenly seemed static.

'So what's one more lie?' She hauled herself to her
feet. Well, it was true, she thought bravely, lifting her
chin as she confronted his solid frame which blocked her
access to the door.

'One too many, Ginny. After a bath and change of
clothes you'll feel refreshed.'

'And if I don't agree to co-operate, I suppose you'll
resort to brute force again?' she challenged, her eyes
darkening with pain.

'Coercion?' Black brows rose in mock-surprise. 'You
do me a grave injustice, Ginny. If you truly prefer us to
stay here for the evening, then we will.'

Every taut line of his body invited her to accept his
challenge, his eyes burning with a blatant hungry desire,

warning her that his veneer of outward calm was the result of a commendable, albeit unreliable self-control.

Ginny swallowed nervously. Steel Anastasi was hungry and it wasn't for food. Power was a formidable aphrodisiac and he was wielding a considerable force, controlling not only the future fortunes of his own father, but that of Sullivan's and its entire small workforce. He was keyed up for conquest, every line of his magnificent body alert, animal instinct and human intelligence combining to create an irresistible force. He didn't love her, but he did want to make love to her. That message was clear and uncomplicated, based solely on the fact that she was a female and close at hand—nothing more.

Every instinct urged her to fight him, physically if necessary. But caution was a powerful curb. Dumbly, painfully, she acknowledged that this was no time for her to become the immovable object of the proverb because, if something had to give, it wouldn't be the man who was standing over her, his face as innocent as a fifteenth-century icon—and they both knew it.

'Give me an hour and I'll be ready to leave,' she said tersely, adding with a sudden flare of defiance, 'But only because Dad's health and happiness depend on your patronage!'

'An excellent and commendable reason.' Steel inclined his head graciously. 'Run along, then, Ginny. I'll lock up and follow you in a few minutes.'

'You aren't going to dictate what I should wear?' She feigned astonishment as she slipped past him and out into the yard.

'You've already turned down my assistance,' he reminded her, his smile following her as she walked away.

'Just dress to please yourself. I'm sure you'll look delightful.'

Not deigning to reply, Ginny forced her tired legs to march away, holding her body erect with a defiant dignity. Safely in the house, she dashed for the bathroom, locking the door firmly behind her. Almost certainly Steel wouldn't breach her privacy, but she wasn't leaving anything to chance.

A twenty-minute soak in the bath had her weariness draining away as she considered what to wear. For one brief, truculent moment she considered putting on her jogging suit, but reason told her it would be a short-lived victory. Steel might have denied any wish to dominate her, but if she didn't dress to his taste she might very well find herself being assisted to do just that. Despite his earlier assertion that her disreputable appearance would increase his father's aggravation and thus enhance his purpose, she hadn't been fooled. Steel might wish to annoy Pandelis—but not at the price of his own pride!

Not that she had much choice, she accorded glumly as, powdered and perfumed, she surveyed the contents of her wardrobe. Nothing in the millionaire class there! Simplicity would have to be the key word. Rather that than be dressed up as if she were some rich man's plaything.

Steel was waiting for her as she entered the living-room. Immediately he rose to his feet, discerning eyes assessing the effect of the multi-coloured silk designer-label halter-neck top she'd bought for a song in a sale, contrasted to the mid-calf length chiffon skirt which swirled about her shapely calves, and which had been a basic ingredient of her wardrobe for the past three years.

On her left wrist she wore the gold cocktail watch her father had bought her for her eighteenth birthday, on the right the delicately fashioned gold bracelet he had given her for her twenty-first. Her only other jewellery was Steel's ring—a splash of opulence against the pale skin of her hand.

The silence was absolute. Waves of panic threatened to demolish her precarious self-esteem as Steel's dark gaze evaluated her, sweeping down the length of her body and back to her face.

So what had he expected? She'd done her best, spent time on a discreet but effective eye make-up, outlined her full mouth with a lipbrush so that its contours were perfectly presented, and brushed her hair into a gleaming swirl of tawny-blonde softness which bounced on her bare shoulders as she moved.

Unable to bear the silence any longer, she blurted out aggressively, 'Well, do I meet with your approval or not?'

'You look bewitching—too bewitching. Before I know it Pandelis will be purring his approval—and that's hardly what I intended!' A mild exasperation put an edge to his voice. 'Now come and drink your coffee and eat the sandwich I've made you. You've got a long night ahead of you.'

An hour later the Lotus drew up smoothly before the elegant entrance of the Iliad Hotel. Tossing his car keys to the doorman, Steel escorted Ginny over the threshold, moving with the brisk steps of a man on familiar territory.

'We'll go up to my apartment first so I can change into another suit.' A firm hand in the small of her back propelled her towards the bank of lifts.

'You have an apartment here? It must cost the earth!' she blurted out in surprise, momentarily forgetting his golden pedigree, as he stood aside to let her enter first before pressing an unmarked button.

'How mercenary you are.' His eyes mocked her. 'I don't claim to rival my sire in riches, but I'm not exactly a pauper. But if extravagance offends you, I plead innocent. Since the hotel belongs to Pandelis, the suite costs me nothing. I find it a convenient base when I'm in London.'

'You're not too proud to live off his bounty, then?' she flashed back sweetly.

'Ah, Ginny, you tempt the devil in me when you question my *philotimo*.' A lively promise of retribution flared in the depths of his sable eyes. 'If it weren't for the fact that I wish you to look your best when I introduce you to Pandelis, you'd surely pay for that comment!' He tucked his hand firmly beneath her arm as the lift came to a halt, leading her down a short corridor. 'The reason I stay here is nothing to do with my being a parasite, but because it frustrates my father to have me physically so near to him yet mentally so distanced!'

'How sad for both of you.' Her spontaneous comment earned her a sharp look, but no verbal retort.

A splendid double door opened easily with the key he drew from his pocket. Standing to one side, he indicated that she should enter.

'Make yourself at home. It'll only take me a few minutes to shower and change.'

How could he have borne giving up such a comfortable and luxurious environment for the lesser pleasures of suburban mediocrity? she wondered in amazement when he'd disappeared through another door and she was able to release her eyes from the broad strength of his retreating back.

Slowly she gazed around the room. Her first impression was one of coolness and space, the carpet a deep French blue, the elegant lounge furniture a shade lighter. One sheet of exquisite Belgian lace covered an enormous picture window at the side of which oyster satin drapes formed swaths of pale colour.

Her quick appraisal took in well-filled bookshelves, a contemporary music centre built into a French walnut casing to match the coffee-tables and a couple of occasional chairs. Two luxurious long-pile rugs in a champagne shade broke up the large carpeted floor area. The plain oyster-coloured silk which covered the walls formed a perfect foil for the scattering of contemporary paintings which graced them.

She was still admiring the pictures, obviously originals, when Steel returned, his lithe body resplendent in a beautifully cut casual suit of oyster-coloured silk, the jacket left open to reveal a mid-brown open-necked shirt.

It was a very Continental look and one, she suspected, that few Englishmen would be able to wear with the panache which typified every aspect of Steel Anastasi's personality. He looked magnificent and her heart seemed to leap into her throat in recognition of the hidden virility which lurked untamed beneath the veneer of sophistication he presented. Unaccountably she shivered.

'Cold, Ginny?' His warm gaze caressed the opaline skin of her naked shoulders. 'Or afraid? If it's the first then you'll soon warm up when we join the rest of the party, if the second—well, just remember I'll be at your side. Shall we go?'

Speechlessly she nodded her head. It wasn't the best reassurance he could have given her!

'So, you're the young woman who thinks she's going to marry my son?'

There was no smile on Pandelis Anastasi's harsh countenance as he stared at Ginny's carefully composed face. A tremor of unease teased the sensitive space between her shoulder-blades as she picked up the hint of aggression underlying the gravelly voice which addressed her. So what had she expected?

As soon as they'd set foot over the threshold of the magnificent flower-bedecked ballroom, as if alerted by radar, Steel's impressive progenitor had espied their entrance. She'd recognised him instantly as he'd deserted the small group surrounding him to shoulder his way through the other guests, probably because the sense of power emanating from him was almost tangible.

For the first time she felt a twinge of real fear. How dangerous was it, she wondered, for Steel to show such open defiance of his father's wishes?

Like the gods whose mythical domain had been his homeland, Pandelis Anastasi would probably stop at nothing to keep his fortune intact, and woe betide anyone who opposed him. This was a man who would know the real meaning of revenge. Somehow she doubted whether sharing his blood would immunise Steel from the full effects of his wrath, should he choose to exercise it.

'Yes.' She found her voice, delighted at its casual coolness. 'Steel has asked me to wear his ring...' That at least was the truth, and she made no attempt to hide the smile which illuminated her eyes in response to her own secret amusement. Emboldened, she added for good measure, 'And I'm proud and happy to do so.' That was a lie. Or was it? Her lashes dropped to disguise the surprise she was sure must be mirrored in her eyes. For an unrehearsed lie the statement had slipped very easily from her normally truthful lips.

'So I see.' Pandelis Anastasi's heavy-lidded eyes dropped to survey her hand, evaluating the cluster of precious stones. 'I don't deny I'm surprised. I confess I suspected my son was amusing himself at my expense when I heard the news—my very great expense, I may add.'

'Don't expect me to shed tears on your behalf, *pateras mou*,' Steel intervened drily, placing a casual, supportive arm round Ginny's shoulders. 'The Greek government is only asking for what you legally owe it. Every man must pay his just dues. I'm sure you'll pay yours willingly, even though the effort will be more painful for you without the connivance of the Stavrolakes family.'

The older man shrugged. 'It's my policy to explore every possible avenue in business. One never knows what is waiting at the end of the road.'

'I'm impressed by your philosophy.' A slight dip of Steel's head accorded his father admiration, but the gleam in his dark eyes lacked the respect to confirm it.

'And I admire the speed and purpose with which you've moved from passive to active defiance of my suggestion.' Pandelis regarded his son with sombre eyes. 'I would have spurred you earlier and harder had I known your defiance would take such an attractive form.'

They were like predator and prey, Ginny thought wildly, and she the minor bait between them. She just wished she could determine which was which.

'So you approve of Ginny?'

Ginny's eyes rose quickly to Steel's face as he posed the question, and she felt his arm round her shoulders tighten possessively; there was a husky intensity in his voice which would have won him an Oscar for his performance, she accorded in silent congratulation. He was calling the older man's bluff, and it was all she could do not to laugh. How galling for him if Pandelis expressed delight that his only son was about to marry a suburban Cinderella! But she wasn't going to stand there docilely to be assessed as if she were some commodity at auction. It wasn't only Greeks who possessed *philotimo*!

'I'd be interested in hearing your opinion on that point too, Mr Anastasi,' she chimed in coolly. But there was nothing either cool or subservient in the way she met the older man's dark, intelligent eyes; nothing humble in the way she lifted her chin and dared him to answer her, the flash of fire in her grey eyes giving them a sparkle which outshone the diamonds on her finger.

'How could I disapprove?' He met her challenge head-on, but there was no pleasure in his expression, only politeness. 'My son has inherited more of my qualities than it pleases him to admit. His taste in women is impeccable. It always has been.'

'Oh!' Ginny drew in a sharp breath. Like the double-headed axe of Minoan culture, Pandelis Anastasi's reply had possessed two deadly cutting surfaces. In one clean blow he'd managed to praise her appearance, at the same time pointing out that she wasn't the first woman to occupy a place in Steel's heart. No, she was wrong. The retort had yet a third blade. It had been intended to remind his son that he and his father had once shared the same lover.

'You must forgive my father, Ginny.' Steel's hand moved caressingly down her bare arm, his voice warm with what sounded like amusement. 'Unfortunately, his command of the English language does not include its finer nuances. I'm sure he didn't mean to insinuate that you are but one of a long line of women who have passed through my life, only that we are both admirers of feminine beauty.'

'Of course,' Pandelis returned smoothly, before turning his hooded gaze to rest appraisingly on Ginny's carefully controlled expression. 'My son is right. My English is more suited to matters of commerce than passion. If I have said anything to mislead you, then I apologise. My son is no less discerning than I myself.' His accent was thick, the words slowly enunciated, the meaning shrouded in ambiguity; but she wasn't fooled. Pandelis Anastasi's command of English was as good as, if not better than, most of the inhabitants of the country! 'The woman my son eventually weds may look forward to a rewarding and lasting relationship, of that I am sure.'

He was letting her know she hadn't fooled him either. Not for one moment. He knew she'd been bought and used. His implication that Steel's 'eventual' bride would enjoy his unwavering faithfulness made it only too clear that he knew it was not she who would be occupying that place.

Pain stabbed briefly at Ginny's heart. Unexpected and demoralising because it wasn't as if she cared a jot for the handsome man who stood at her side, an enigmatic smile turning the corners of his tender mouth! Only the strength of her will-power kept the bright smile painted on her mouth as the elder Anastasi released her from his scrutiny to turn his unsmiling eyes on his son, addressing Steel in rapid, guttural Greek.

To Ginny's ear the language lacked the soft musicality of Italian, or the rhythmical cadence of Spanish. Relegated to watching Steel's face as he apparently faced a barrage of questions, she tried to discern his reactions. At times he seemed amused, at others angry, but it was difficult to judge. To her untuned ear the conversation sounded harsh and unfriendly.

'Forgive me, *agape mou*.' At last Steel returned his attention to her. 'My father meant no discourtesy by excluding you from our conversation. As he himself admits, his English is not proficient enough to deal with the full expression of his emotions.'

There was nothing on that bland, beautifully hewn face to give her a clue, but she knew perfectly well that Pandelis's emotions had been broadcast in Greek because he was aware that she didn't understand the language—which meant they'd been even less flattering than those he'd voiced to date!

'Of course I understand.' It was a game she could play as well as the two men who were treating her as a pawn in a contest in which neither would ever be the winner. Calling up an acting ability she'd never realised she possessed, she simpered sweetly, fluttering her eyelashes at Steel. 'English is such a *limited* tongue, isn't it? But the Greeks always have a word for it—isn't that how the saying goes?'

'How erudite of you, beloved!' Steel's black eyes laughed into her upturned face with obvious approval.

'In this case the words my father found more easily spoken in his native tongue consisted of a welcome into our family, allied to an expression of deep regret that his present wife, my stepmother, was unable to fly over at such short notice to meet you on this happy occasion, but looks forward to redressing the matter shortly.'

'How sweet!' She was channelling her pain into a perverse pleasure, holding out her hand artlessly towards the older man. 'I'd like to believe that our announcement has contributed to the enjoyment of your name-day.'

Pandelis didn't speak; instead he took her hand, and to her astonishment raised it to his lips, brushing the back lightly against his lips. When he lowered it she thought she glimpsed a grudging but unmistakable gleam of respect lurking in the depth of his piercing eyes.

The next couple of hours passed in a blur as Steel guided her away from his father's awesome presence to introduce her to friends and acquaintances whose names she would never remember. Pinning a smile on her face, she shook hands, exchanged pleasantries and accepted congratulations which seemed well-meant if a little incredulous. Not that she blamed them for that. Who in their right mind would believe that Steel Anastasi would fall in love with Leo Sullivan's daughter when his own world was peopled with women of such beauty, glamour and wealth?

When Steel eventually led her to the extensive buffet which had been prepared at one end of the ballroom, she discovered to her surprise that her ordeal had sharpened her appetite. Contrary to her expectations she found no difficulty in eating the delicious food, especially when she was able to wash it down with a glass or two of fragrant Greek wine.

It was later, much later, when the bouzouki band played and the dancing began, that her fragile control began to slip. The music was romantic, the lights low, and several other couples were dancing, intent only on their own pleasure, as Steel drew her into his arms, pulling her close against his own warm, hard form, arousing an agony of need to life within her ungiven body, and he led her to the cleared area at the centre of the room.

Driven by a warm flood of feeling which ebbed and flowed through every molecule of her being, Ginny raised her hands and drifted them lightly against the strong column of Steel's neck as they swayed together, feeling a shiver of expectation in the warm, pulsating flesh beneath her palm. When Steel dipped his head, his mouth finding her cheek, his soft lips nibbling at the naked lobe of her ear, she sighed rapturously, a small moan escaping her as she inhaled the sharp, clean scent of his skin.

A mindless, shameful ecstasy was storming her traitorous body as she fought to retain her self-control. Dear heavens! What was happening to her? How could she possibly respond to the expertise of a man who cared nothing for her? A man who despised her emotions and abilities and who had used her in the most callous way? A man whose interest in her was carnal and opportunist?

There was only one answer to all those questions and it drove the breath from her body as it hit her. Steel Anastasi, that arch-manipulator, had thrust his way into her life, destroying everything: her hopes, her values and her plans. But worse, far worse, he'd broken down the barriers she had erected against him and stolen her heart. Horrified by the revelation, she missed the beat of the rhythm and had to clutch at his arms as she was caught off balance. She could neither understand nor deny it, but the truth was evident. She was in love with him.

As panic followed the path lit by desire, she fought to find a means of destroying the heady magic which was entrancing her! Somehow she conjured up enough strength to alter her grip on Steel's upper arms, pushing herself away, levering enough space between them to gaze up into the liquid darkness of his magnificent eyes.

'What did Pandelis really say about me?' She asked the first question which entered her mind.

'You really want to know?' And then, as she nodded vigorously, 'Very much what you would expect in the circumstances: that I am a very lucky man to find a woman who is prepared to tolerate my obstinacy and ingratitude; that it is high time I took on domestic responsibility...' He paused, his narrowed eyes agleam with amusement.

'Yes?' she prompted, guessing that there was a sting in the tail—or did she mean tale?—still to come, and, bracing herself for another of the elder Anastasi's barbed remarks, she demanded, 'Then what did he say?'

Steel laughed softly. 'He asked me if you were *enghios*—expecting my child.'

CHAPTER TEN

'OH!'

Unaccountably Ginny was shocked—which was absurd, because from Pandelis Anastasi's point of view it was a very sensible question. No wonder he'd reverted to his own language, though!

Neither was she sure she liked the look on Steel's face as he enlightened her. She discerned an element of gloating in his deep-set eyes, which had registered and were enjoying her dismay. Had he accepted his father's prognosis? An engagement to a woman of another race might not be held sacrosanct—but imminent fatherhood...

'I hope you disillusioned him!' she expostulated sternly, trying without success to detach herself completely from his firm grip, his soft chuckle at her helplessness doing nothing to reassure her.

'Relax, Ginny... I told him you were as pure as the day I first met you.' There was an odd inflexion in the statement that puzzled her, but she had no time to analyse it before he added softly, 'I told him he'd have to wait a little while longer before we could present him with his first grandchild.'

His silent laughter mocked her as he moved his hand in a sensual caress across her bare shoulders. The last thing she wanted to think of was bearing Steel's child, yet the intimacy his suggestion conjured in her imagination made her mouth go dry with fearful anticipation.

Summoning up every last atom of self-respect, she managed to raise a supercilious eyebrow, at the same time faking a yawn, delicately covering her mouth with her hand before returning carelessly, 'A *lot* longer would have been more honest! Really, Steel, don't you think we've milked this situation enough? I'm very tired and I'd like to go home.'

'My own thoughts exactly.'

Not expecting such ready agreement, she was delighted when in the space of a few minutes she found herself neatly extricated from the gathering after delivering a brief farewell to Pandelis, and seated in the Lotus.

Only when Steel turned on the ignition and she sensed the atmosphere between them, thick with tension, did she realise the magnitude of her mistake. Desperately she sought to make conversation, her frantic mind seizing on the first question which occurred to it.

'Shouldn't we have taken your father a gift?' she asked brightly.

'If we'd been in Greece I suppose we could have taken him a goat or a lamb.' His profile was an unreadable mask, as if her question had irritated him. 'But I suspect the Iliad thinks too highly of its expensive carpets to have welcomed such an expression of our regard. In any case,' he added after a short pause, 'in one respect you could say we did abide by tradition. You are, after all, the sacrificial lamb in this little drama—are you not?'

Melodrama more likely! she thought sourly, but his comment wasn't conducive to further conversation. Rather than dignify it by a reply, she turned her gaze to look out of the side-window. What could she have said, anyway? She felt like Cinderella after the ball, but in her case the prince was still with her, and the temptation to believe and enjoy the fantasy of being loved by him was becoming increasingly harder to resist. She closed her eyes, her long lashes fanning darkly against her pale skin. Once she was home and in her own room she'd be out of harm's way.

The drive home was fast and uneventful, her pretence of sleep an excuse to avoid conversation. As the Lotus entered Leo's driveway she determined to make one last desperate effort to barricade herself against the potent threat posed by Steel's proximity.

Faking a yawn, she tapped her hand politely across her lips, before easing her body against the soft upholstery as if to loosen it from the stiffness of sleep.

'There's absolutely no need for you to spend the night here, Steel.' Pleased with the bored note she'd managed to introduce into her voice, she continued in the same mode, 'I'm afraid Dad's a little over-protective where I'm concerned. The few break-ins round here have been opportunist and in the daytime, and the house is well-protected with locks and bolts. You might as well go back and spend a comfortable night at the Iliad.'

'And break my promise to your father?' A hint of censure deepened his voice. 'Besides, what on earth would Pandelis think if he discovered you'd thrown me out?'

She refused to answer the question, turning her head away, but not before she'd observed the smile of smug satisfaction which lifted the corners of his mouth.

What had she expected? she asked herself resignedly. But he hadn't cornered the market on pride! She might have to suffer his presence in the house, but there was no law which said she needed to spend time in his company! As soon as he brought the car to a standstill, she was out and letting herself into the house, walking quickly through the hall intent on summoning Kefi in for the night and feeding him. The little cat was waiting for her and it took only minutes to put down fresh food and milk for him and ensure that his basket was where he liked it. Now all she had to do was call out 'good-night' and make for the sanctuary of her bedroom.

Her misapprehension was dispelled the moment she poked her head round the door of the gently lit living-room, the rehearsed words withering on her tongue as Steel advanced towards her. She hesitated that one moment too long, allowing him to gather her to him, his hands capturing her face and turning it towards him as he gazed down at her.

All thought of resistance froze in her brain as her eyes drank in the message written in every line of his face, in each taut muscle of his expressive body. If he'd been a starving man sighting sustenance for the first time in many days his purpose could not have been more clearly mirrored in his smouldering, hungry eyes.

'Steel,' she whispered, his name dying on her lips as he brushed a kiss across her warm, newly responsive mouth. It was a tentative caress, a playful tribute, but behind it lay a simmering passion only just held in control.

Some residue of reserve whispered that she should struggle, but her mouth was longing for a repetition of the tender pleasure it had just tasted and her skin was burning with expectation as his predatory hands caressed the silk and chiffon that hid her body from his penetrating eyes.

'You did very well tonight, Ginny,' he told her softly. 'Pandelis really fell for your performance.'

'Then he took it very well,' she observed wryly, her heart beating an urgent tattoo as her nervous system responded to the scent of Steel's skin, the pressure of his seductive palms as they caressed her pliant body.

'Because he knows when he's beaten,' he murmured against her ear.

'Then he's a better loser than you led me to expect!' She laughed nervously, lowering her gaze to glimpse at the whisper-soft chiffon of her skirt, before turning her cheek to avoid the onslaught of his plundering mouth.

Keep talking, she thought wildly. Anything to keep him at a distance while she gathered her crumbling defences. This wasn't what she wanted. It couldn't be what she wanted . . . could it?

'Such graciousness to an English waif when he expected a Greek heiress as his daughter-in-law!' she opined lightly, shrugging her shoulders and lifting her chin nonchalantly. Instantly she realised her mistake, because the action had drawn his gaze to the nervous little pulse beating in her throat, the untrammelled line of her shoulders, pearly pink beneath the multi-coloured swath of her halter neckline.

'Like you, he's full of surprises, and not all of them bad.' A swift inner amusement lit the hard onyx of Steel's eyes with a purpose so dangerously sensual that Ginny, forewarned, instinctively backed away, only to find herself imprisoned by his fingers, which caught and tightened around her wrist. 'We Greeks are proud of our heritage but history shows that our blood is often enriched by that of women from different cultures.'

'But not by that of men?' she demanded, seizing an opportunity to distract him while she tried to restore her own crumbling defences.

His thumbs caressed the soft skin of her inner wrist. 'That rarely happens. Perhaps because Greek men are such passionate lovers, hmm?'

'I wouldn't know.' Ginny tried to make the response sound carelessly indifferent, but the sudden knot in her diaphragm caused her voice to tremble. 'It's very late and I've had a long day, so if you'll excuse me I'm going up to my room.' She tried to speak calmly, but her racing pulse betrayed her as she tried to disengage her wrists from the steady pressure of Steel's marauding thumbs.

An unbidden thought sprang to her mind. All those willing but too demanding women in his life—did their hearts thunder like this when he held them? Did they suffer from tremors like those which were trembling down her spine?

'What a good idea, *agape mou*.' Seductively low, he breathed the words, the warmth of his body infiltrating hers, intent on conquering the last pockets of her resistance with the determination of an invading army bent on victory. 'Shall we go there together?'

He held her against him, locked in his embrace, the brooding sensuality mirrored in his beautiful eyes a dark threat, more intimidating than the huskily voiced question.

'That's not what I meant...' Her voice shook as her brain clicked into a last desperate burst of activity. Some latent energy blazing into life in the cause of self-preservation, she seized on the lie she'd always intended Steel to believe. 'You'll never take Howard's place.

You've destroyed my future with him, but you'll never destroy my love.'

She felt him recoil as the impact of her cry hit him, then he was lifting one hand from her waist to imprison her chin, lifting it with firm fingers, tilting it so that she was forced to gaze on the hard, chiselled planes of his face. 'Well, that's fine by me, Ginny.' She winced as the electricity from his touch ran like a chain of fire through her blood. 'What I'm thinking about has nothing to do with love. I'm not asking to replace Howard in your heart. I'm happy to settle for replacing him in your bed.'

Ignoring her gasp of rejection, he released her jaw, sliding his hand across her shoulders to mould her aroused body against his own, dragging her hard against him, his strength ridiculing her puny efforts to prevent him as he covered her mouth with his own.

Further resistance was useless as his mouth recaptured hers, his tongue tracing the fullness of her lips, begging acceptance into the soft recesses of her mouth.

No longer a stranger in his arms, Ginny was beset by waves of desire, her body recognising and responding to the familiar scent of his skin and the warm, moist texture of his mouth. The last citadel of her defiance crumbled before his onslaught as, forsaking all pretence, she surrendered to the inevitable, responding to the relentless demands of his voracious mouth with the savage, erotic passion he had conjured to life within her, expelling a small mew of pleasure as disturbing but delightful pangs of anguish assailed her loins.

Dear heaven but she wanted him! Hypnotised by the power of the hormones flooding her blood, she made no protest when he moved urgent fingers to seek the fullness of her breast. Instead she arched spontaneously towards him, every fibre of her being craving the pleasure he promised her.

'Ginny...' He breathed her name against her skin, his lips damp with the taste of her. 'This will be better upstairs.'

She heard the words but couldn't answer their implicit question. Her heart was thundering too hard against his, and she was too conscious of his powerful muscles and sinews tautened with the desire which raged through his virile frame to think rationally.

'Ginny?'

Her name alone, soft and sweet like honey dripping from a spoon, reminded her that he was waiting for her agreement.

From out of nowhere panic seized her. A rising hysteria forced her to oppose the seductive pressure of his mouth against the delicate flare of her cheekbones. Blindly she raised her hands against his collarbones in a desperate attempt to lever herself away from him.

'No,' she whispered, her voice ensnared in her throat.

'Why not?' His voice was slurred, the pupils of his eyes so dilated with desire that they appeared black. 'You want me as badly as I want you. Trust me, Ginny, I would never put you in any danger.'

With every cell in her body clamouring for his possession, only pride restrained her. He didn't even like her—let alone love her! A bitter laugh rose in her diaphragm, choking to stillness in her throat. Howard, who'd considered marriage to her, had never shown signs of a burning desire to possess her body. Steel, who had dismissed her mind and personality as unworthy of him, was greedy to enjoy her flesh. Bitterness rose like sap in spring. He'd guaranteed to protect her from danger, but the only peril he could preserve her from was physical. No protection would repair the damage he'd already inflicted on her heart.

Aware that he was still waiting for her answer, she tried to assemble her thoughts, her hands flattened against his chest, trying to hold him at bay, the diamonds of the ring he'd lent her catching the only light available to sparkle like a glow-worm against the pale sleeve of his suit. Then suddenly logic was not enough, and there was only one possible answer.

'Because,' she said simply, 'my knees have gone so weak I don't think I could climb the stairs.'

Steel accepted her invitation as she'd known he would. One arm beneath her armpits, the other beneath her knees, he swept her off her feet, taking the stairs two at a time, so that she gasped at the sheer velocity of movement, her arms linked around his neck to preserve her balance. Her own bedroom door stood slightly ajar and he thrust it open with one shoulder.

Her stomach clenching in nervous excitement, Ginny reached to entwine her fingers in the thick dark thatch of his hair as he began to unbutton the front fastening of her halter-top, his powerful male fingers showing a surprising dexterity as they dealt with the small, slippery buttons. At last she succumbed to her own needs, a small moan of pleasure escaping her lips as, his task finished, Steel brushed the halter free from her neck, allowing it to slide down her pale shoulders to fall in a crumpled heap of multi-coloured silk to the floor.

The sharp inhalation of his breath as the action revealed the deep cleavage of her breasts above the strapless bra, which had been the only possible garment she could have worn beneath it, acted as a powerful aphrodisiac, so that she swayed towards him eagerly as he lowered his head and his mouth sought to savour the perfumed skin he'd revealed.

Tentatively Ginny gave in to her own desires, reaching out her hands to welcome him, sliding her palms beneath his jacket, the clamour in her blood increasing as his low-pitched groan acknowledged the convulsive clutching of her fingers as they slid beneath his jacket and shirt to move against his warm golden skin.

'Wait...' His breathed instruction was little more than a sigh as with a sharp movement he shed his jacket, tossing it in the direction of her bedroom chair to which it clung briefly before sliding to the thick rose-red carpet, and, with a hand that trembled, he found and released the catch of her bra.

The cool air touched her naked, heated skin before Steel did, then he was fondling her with worshipping fingers, burying his face in her fullness, only raising his mouth from the opaline slopes of her breasts to travel it along her throat, following the clean, clear line of her jaw, saluting it with tender, controlled kisses interrupted only by his need to speak.

'Tell me you want me, Ginny. Touch me, show me how much...'

Warmth surged through her at his husky, disjointed plea. Caught up in a maelstrom of emotion too powerful to rationalise, she was shocked by the power of her own response to his ardent words.

Blurred with passion, Steel's voice was as seductive as the practised predatory fingers, whose expertise had already brought the responsive tips of her breasts to hard, erectile splendour. She wanted him so much, wanted to feel his hard male mouth softening in adulation over every inch of her naked body, wanted him so desperately to love her as no other man ever had.

She was breathing rapidly as his gaze locked with hers. It was the face of a stranger, transfigured by desire— basic male appetite unashamedly blatant. For a fraction of a second fear laid an icy hand on her heart. Would her untried body disappoint him? Leave him unsatisfied and her humiliated?

But her love for him had grown to an all-consuming flame, devouring her body, burning her with a fire that only he could quench. What matter he didn't love her? He desired her and she loved him. It was more than enough.

So when he dragged the buttons of his shirt through the buttonholes, her eager fingers swept the garment from his shoulders, avid to touch and enjoy the smooth, firm muscles of his torso, her eyes alight with pleasure as she recalled the first time she'd seen and touched his satin skin, ensuring that Kefi's claws had left no scar. She'd served him well on that occasion, she thought. She wouldn't disappoint him now.

When he eased her gently on to the bed, guiding her with his own body, she shifted her position to his command, helping him to undress her, offering her body joyously to him for their mutual pleasure.

At first the soft physical caresses he lavished on her tender, receptive skin were comforting, and then suddenly not comforting at all but wildly disturbing. Her own fingers, which had initially explored his exposed flesh with delicate perception, became more demanding, moving with a hungry appreciation of the muscled strength beneath their caress.

Above her his face hovered, deep-set eyes heavy-pupilled with desire. 'Do you want me to love you, Ginny?' he asked, the words disjointed and laboured. 'Because if you don't, now is the time to tell me.'

'I want you to.' Her reply slid out between lips warm and aching to be repossessed.

'Then show me, *agape mou*... If you want me as much as I want you, show me...'

Perhaps he still didn't trust her reactions, or perhaps he liked his women to take the initiative. Either way it was an invitation she had no intention of rejecting. Moving her hands to the catch at his waist, feeling his deep shudder, she heard his harsh cry of anticipation as she fumbled with desperate fingers at the unwieldy zip, trying with impatient fingers to free it, to render him as naked and shameless to her eyes as she was to his.

Impatiently he came to her aid, removing the final barriers between them. She was dissolving with expectation, burning and shaking, so sensitive that her naked skin twitched away from his exploring touch.

As if at a great distance she heard her own voice sobbing his name over and over again, then he was releasing her from her agony, lowering his body to cover her, replacing the pain of denial with that of fulfillment.

In her ignorance she hadn't expected the violent power of his possession. The act of love, primeval and creative, gathered together her scattered senses, grounded her flying fantasies, concentrated her whole being on the thrust and vigour of the beautiful male body which bucked above her.

Her pleasure that first time was in knowing how deeply satisfying Steel found the tight, warm sheath of her body, allied to the joy of being united with the man she loved, as she caught his rhythm and moved to meet and match his need.

Eventually his body left her, but she could still feel him deep inside her. Hugging the knowledge to herself, she prayed for the sensation to linger, so that later, when she was alone, she could recall his pleasure and his passion.

'Why me, Ginny? Why did you give yourself to me, when no other man had ever loved you?' Steel's harsh voice shattered her lethargy.

Still bathed in a rosy glow of happiness, she wasn't prepared for his reaction as he dragged himself up on one elbow to regard her with unsmiling eyes.

What kind of question was that? Struggling to sit up, suddenly self-conscious beneath his gimlet-eyed appraisal, she reached to cover her body with her discarded skirt, crumpling the soft chiffon against her newly tender breasts. Astonished that he'd even noticed such a technicality as her virginity, since she'd no clear recollection of experiencing any discomfort, she regarded his set face with dismay.

'I—I don't understand what you mean,' she faltered, then as a glimmer of comprehension filtered through into her dazed mind, 'You don't imagine I was trying to put you under any obligation!' Heat coloured her cheeks at the idea.

'What I thought,' he informed her tersely, 'was that you and Howard had been lovers. Damn it, Ginny—I never expected to find you were untouched!'

'Damn your expectations, then!' Furiously she glared up into his accusing face. 'How dare you assume anything of the kind?'

'Because Howard was your fiancé! Because you were going to Rome with him! What was I supposed to think?'

'How do I know?' She stared at him with mounting consternation, hurt beyond belief that he was systematically destroying the memory of an experience she'd been determined to enshrine in her heart forever. 'That my father had brought me up to follow old-fashioned principles? That I put more value on my body's integrity than to offer it around as carelessly as I'd offer cakes at a party? That Howard respected my feelings?' Her breath sawed harshly, angrily, in her throat. 'I'm sorry, Steel, but I wasn't expecting a post-mortem on my performance. If it disappointed you, then I can only apologise!'

She started to get up, but found herself pushed back as Steel pinned her down into the pillows by her shoulders, his naked body a potent threat as his eyes blazed down at her.

'Post-mortem be damned, Ginny! Your father is my friend. Where I come from a man doesn't take the virginity of his friend's daughter. If I'd known the truth I wouldn't have touched you,' he retorted bleakly.

Guilt made his face still and remote, his cold rejection arousing an answering anger in Ginny's heart.

'Well, since you didn't,' she shot back, 'you needn't feel guilty. I'm hardly likely to tell Dad what happened, am I? Besides, there has to be a first time in every woman's life, and, since you robbed Howard of that privilege, you were the obvious candidate to take his place.' Her stormy eyes warred with his as she continued with quiet deliberation, 'Particularly since you claimed to have been well-tutored in the art of love.'

Dark colour scorched his cheekbones at her dismissive verdict. Pushing himself away from her, he unfolded his length to stalk away from the bed, proud and unashamed in his powerful masculinity, leaving her to stare at his uncompromising back view as he rescued his discarded clothes and dextrously covered his nudity.

When he turned and spoke again his voice was harsh. 'I hope my performance came up to your expectations, then, Ginny, because from the moment I violated you all pretence between us ceased. All that remains now is to name the day for our wedding.'

'Don't be ridiculous!' she flared angrily. 'Look, I won't be put through the third degree——'

'You'll be put through more than that, Ginny.' His expressive eyes were glacial, his voice sharp and uncompromising. 'Because I'm afraid you're not going to escape the consequences of your curiosity. I intend to fulfil my obligations to you and your family and make you my wife as soon as Leo is fit to give you to me.'

'What utter rubbish!' Horrified, Ginny stared at his implacable face. He had to be joking! A contrived betrothal was one thing—a contrived wedding something totally different. 'The whole idea's absurd. I've no intention of marrying you just because you were my first lover!'

'Your only lover,' he corrected smoothly. 'Virginity in a woman is a prize I happen to value and one I have no intention of discarding. You made a bad error, Ginny, when you chose me to understudy Howard, and you're going to have to learn to live with the consequences.' The belligerent echo of his voice softened slightly. 'But I promise I'll make them as pleasurable as I can.'

'You'd have to carry me down the aisle!' she snapped, her emotions spinning out of control as mortification replaced the heady rapture of desire satiated.

'A task well within my capabilities.' A glitter of malicious delight warmed the sable depths of his eyes. 'But unnecessary, because, while your father would have accepted our joint decision to part, it would break his heart to learn that the two of us connived to cheat him.'

'You mean you'd tell him?' She stared at him aghast, stiff with hurt and bewilderment.

'Not me, Ginny—you.' He appraised her pale face impatiently. 'What other option would you have for explaining why you'd changed your mind?'

'I'd think of something,' she said sullenly. 'Anything to avoid being tied to a man who felt forced to surrender his bachelor status to satisfy his own pride.' She shuddered, realising too late that she should have been less observant of the truth. How much better to have said 'to a man I don't love,' but, with her body still slaked by his fullness, the lie had come too late to her mind.

'Ah, if that's all that bothers you, then rest easy, *agape mou*.' His narrow stare was unnerving. 'Marriage was always on my agenda when the circumstances were right.'

'You call these right?' She glowered at him in disbelief.

He shrugged careless shoulders. 'It's about time I established my own household instead of living in hotels. Given time, I've little doubt you'll make a dutiful and compliant wife and mother. In return, I shall try to be a considerate husband. Many successful marriages have been founded on shakier bases than those.'

A suffocating sensation burned in Ginny's throat. Was there no reasoning with the brute?

'But not mine,' she riposted tersely. 'I'll marry for love or not at all.'

'Spinsterhood won't suit you, Ginny—and if you're hoping Howard will pick up the pieces, forget it. He doesn't love you—not as you need to be loved. He never did. If you're honest with yourself you'll admit it.'

Despite the warmth of the room Ginny shivered. Of course she admitted it. But Howard wasn't the only man in her life not to love her. Steel despised her. From the moment he'd stepped across the threshold of her office she'd sensed his animosity. He'd amused himself by frustrating every attempt she'd made to rescue Sullivan's herself, ridiculed her very presence on the premises, and then, humiliatingly, used her body for his own pleasure, and finally, instead of treating what happened with the *savoir-faire* of a practised playboy, he'd insulted her by expecting her to fall over herself to spend the rest of her life at his side.

'You're wasting your time, and I'm tired.' Bitterness rose like gall to leave an acrid taste in her mouth. 'I'd like you to leave.'

For a moment he studied her drawn face intently, then, to her surprise, he nodded.

'Perhaps that would be for the best.' He accepted her rejection with every sign of equanimity. 'And in the meantime might I recommend you get a good night's sleep, Ginny. You look as if you need it.'

CHAPTER ELEVEN

As A parting shot it stung without inflicting mortal injury. Ginny waited for Steel to leave the room before slumping down on the bed. No one had ever told her that love, like a well-cut diamond, had many facets. How was it possible to feel anger and resentment against a man and yet want nothing more than to melt into his arms, surrender one's body to his careless caresses?

She wrapped her arms round herself comfortingly, hugging her upper body, forcing herself to concentrate on the good things in her life—the improvement in her father's condition, the future security of Sullivan's.

On the debit side were her feelings, the emotions which Steel Anastasi had callously evoked, using her with a master game-player's touch to further his own interests. He'd used her and she'd been a willing tool, but for how much longer could she bear to share his existence now that she loved him?

Emotionally and physically exhausted, she pulled the covers of the bed down, hauling herself beneath the sheets, hunching her body in the foetal position like a baby seeking the reassurance of the womb. Later she would shower and find her clean nightdress; now she only wanted to huddle in the dark comfort of the bed, the imprint of Steel's body on her own both agony and ecstasy.

Instead she dropped into an uneasy sleep, fitfully interrupted by vivid dreams where she was lost in a foreign

country, or stranded deep in subterranean passages with
no indications of exit. When a brisk knock on her door
brought her to the consciousness of the dawn of a
beautiful summer day, her first emotion was one of relief
that she was safe, promptly followed by apprehension
as the memories of the previous evening's débâcle
flooded her consciousness and she realised it was Steel
demanding entrance.

'Just a moment!' Pulling herself upright, she combed
her fingers through her dishevelled hair, before pulling
the sheet up to cover her body, holding its edges against
her shoulders. Embarrassed by the knowledge that her
face still bore traces of last night's make-up and bitterly
ashamed that Steel would realise how disturbed she'd
been by what had happened between them, she wished
whole-heartedly that she'd made the effort to drag herself
along to the bathroom the previous night. Too late now,
she accepted resignedly as another series of raps broke
the silence of the early morning.

'You can come in if you must,' she called out, not
bothering to conceal the irritation in her voice.

'Good morning to you, too.' Steel entered, a mug of
steaming coffee in one hand, his voice and appearance
bland. Just as if nothing out of the ordinary had happened last night! But then, perhaps for him, it hadn't.

Dark eyes swept over her with the speed and accuracy
of a laser scanner, registering every detail of her appearance. To be used in evidence during the trial she
would be facing over the coming days? she wondered.

'Thank you,' she muttered ungraciously, painfully
aware of the contrast between her own unkempt appearance and the pristine vision of Steel in immaculate
suit, shirt and tie.

'Are you all right, Ginny?' There was a strange tenderness in the question which caught at her heart.

'Absolutely fine.' The lie came glibly to her tongue as she reached over to take the mug from the bedside table, inhaling the fragrance of its contents with deep pleasure before raising it to her parched mouth and taking a welcome sip, refusing to amplify her answer. She had nothing to add to what she'd told Steel the previous evening.

'Good, because I'm afraid I'm going to have to leave you to your own devices today, *agape mou*. There are several matters of business which need my urgent attention. I intend to deal with them as quickly as possible, to leave myself free to deal with the arrangements for our wedding.' Seemingly blissfully unaware of Ginny's swift inhalation of frustration, he glanced down at his watch, continuing smoothly, 'As you see, I'm making an early start, but both Duncan and Cathy have their instructions and, should anything unforeseen occur, a message can be left for me at the Iliad—if I'm not available someone there will know where to contact me.'

He paused, his handsome brow quilted into a frown. 'Was there anything else? Ah, yes. I've fed Kefi and let him out in the garden.' Narrowed eyes surveyed her critically. 'You look as if you could use some fresh air and sunshine too, Ginny. Why not drive down to the coast and get a suntan for your wedding-day?'

Lifting her head proudly to meet his ingenuous gaze, Ginny felt a cold sweat break out all over her body. Every grain of reason was urging her to reiterate her opposition to his absurd plans, but he was too close, too dangerously alert for her to take the chance of igniting the fires which she sensed lay just beneath the surface of his civilised demeanour. He was spoiling for a fight and he held all the advantages. Not only was he sparkling with health, vigour and the energy provided by the breakfast he'd undoubtedly made for himself, but he had the physical and psychological superiority of being fully clothed!

Tamping down her vexation, she forced her mouth into a smile. Agreement would surely be the fastest means of getting him out of the bedroom!

'I might just do that,' she agreed sweetly, and saw from the quick shadow which crossed his face that her apparent docility hadn't fooled him for a moment.

'Wise girl.' Too late she read his intention, shrinking away as he moved swiftly to perch on the edge of the bed, one arm encircling her naked back, drawing her against him, the other hand grasping her chin lightly, turning her face towards his own.

'Don't...' She was torn between the choice of protecting her modesty or submitting to Steel's kiss, and her fingers released the sheet as she raised her arms to fend him off. 'I haven't showered...' she began to protest in horror, only to have the words stilled in her mouth as Steel's lips made contact, assaulting her senses. Gently, eloquently, they moved like the caress of warm velvet, kindling a blaze of response deep within her, so that her breath came shallow and fast, and all thought of opposing him withered and died.

Automatically her hands rose, not in defence now but in welcome, lacing round his neck, so that her breasts were crushed against the expensive silk cloth of his jacket and she could feel his heavy heartbeat thundering against her own breastbone. When he deepened the kiss, she gave herself up totally to the unrelenting demands of his marauding mouth.

It was over too soon and he was easing away from her, detaching her hands from his neck, stepping away to stare down at her with patronising satisfaction reflected in his dark pupils.

'You smell and taste delicious, Ginny. As a woman should.' He sighed in mock-despair. 'I see you have a lot to learn if you believe a man prefers a scrubbed and sanitised woman to one endowed with her own sensual perfume. But it could be a long lesson and one that will have to wait until I have more time to devote to it.'

Ashamed and confused by the havoc he'd wrought on her, Ginny could only cower back as he leaned towards her to run a finger over her parted, pulsating lips. 'I'll try not to stay away too long.'

She was still trying to come to terms with her own unexpected and humiliating capitulation when he let himself out of her bedroom, closing the door gently behind him.

At the start of the day she'd had no intention of following Steel's suggestion that she spend some time on the coast, but, having spent the greater part of the morning with her father, it had seemed a good idea. Leo Sullivan's greatly improved condition and his obvious eagerness to return to work, coupled with his continued enthusiasm about her supposed plans to marry Steel, had left her feeling emotionally exhausted.

Now, driving back to Taychapel along the A24, she could contemplate the time spent at the pleasant seaside resort at Worthing with pleasure. At least it had been better than mooning about the house or embarrassing

Cathy and Duncan with her unwanted presence in the office.

Damn Steel! she thought bitterly. He'd trapped her in a position from which she could escape only with the maximum of difficulty and unpleasantness, not to say gross disappointment as far as her father was concerned. Yet escape she would, because the alternative was untenable. She'd only just faced up to the truth about her feelings for Howard. She wasn't about to trap herself in another disastrous liaison just because Steel Anastasi's Greek pride demanded it!

If the latter lusted after a sweet-scented female in his bed, then he would have to look elsewhere, she determined with an untypical stab of pique. By his own admission it wouldn't be a difficult search. After all, it wasn't as if she, Ginny, could possibly become pregnant from their brief but passionate coupling. True to his word, Steel had ensured that she'd been protected from every kind of harm—save one. Her bitter laugh echoed inside the car. There was a fortune waiting for the person who could invent a protective sheath against a broken heart!

Wearied by the repetitive train of her thoughts, she flicked on the car radio, pressing the button for pre-set stations, seeking something with rhythm and beat which might serve to raise her spirits. At the third attempt she caught the end of a news item and was about to search for another wavelength when the reporter began to speak again. Her hands tightened round the steering-wheel in disbelief at the coincidence as she heard the smooth voice continue, 'After today's surprise news that the ailing Marsons Supermarket Group has been taken over by European-based Anastasi Holdings, we have Mr Pandelis

Anastasi, chairman and managing director of the conglomerate, here in the studio with us.

'Mr Anastasi, you're well-known as an entrepreneur and a major force in the leisure and catering trade, but supermarkets—this is something of a new undertaking for you, surely?'

An odd feeling of impending disaster taking hold of her heart, Ginny forced herself to stay calm as Pandelis's gravelly voice came over the airwaves.

'I regard it as a logical expansion. Marsons has a foothold in many high streets but, unfortunately, is suffering from the twin faults of underfunding and complacency, two effects I intend to change immediately. One of my first moves will be to invigorate the chain's existing house and garden centres by introducing a whole new range of products intended for interior design, under the brand name of Orchid.'

Orchid! But that was impossible! Sullivan's had sole rights to distribution in the UK. Without their major supplier they were finished. The deadline for achieving minimum sales might be approaching fast but it certainly hadn't expired! Until it did, the franchise remained theirs.

A terrible nausea seized Ginny as the exuberant Greek continued expansively, 'There's a large, mainly untapped market for imitation plants, trees and flowers of the quality only Orchid International can supply. I see the expansion of this element as not only a lucrative business project, but also as an opportunity to improve the environment.'

Oh, dear God! What was going on? If Pandelis had made some unholy alliance with Orchid it had to be illegal.

Blinking rapidly in an effort to clear the tears of anger which had temporarily misted her eyes, she forced herself to continue listening, sucking her breath in in chagrin as the interviewer continued, 'Despite rumours linking his name with shipping heiress Irene Stavrolakes, your only son has recently announced his intention of marrying an unknown English girl. Are you disappointed with his choice?'

Oh, how dared they discuss her over the air, as if she were some commodity for sale over the counter? Ginny pressed her foot down on the accelerator, urging the Renault up to the legal limit as Pandelis's guttural voice echoed round the car.

'Not at all. I'm delighted with my son's choice of a wife. Ginette Sullivan is a beautiful young woman who will bring into the family, among other undoubted advantages, new blood and vitality.'

'Other advantages.' Ginny paled as realisation dawned, her hand shaking as it gripped the steering-wheel. There was only one way Pandelis could have got his hands on the vital Orchid franchise—through his son. In a position of trust, Steel had informed Orchid that Sullivan's was unable to meet its contractual commitment and Pandelis had been waiting beside the fertile field her father had ploughed and sown to gather in the harvest.

Suddenly everything was clear. This was why Steel had been prepared to put up such a large sum of money in order to gain her father's confidence; why, when the older man had initially refused to accept his investment, he'd been forced to seize on the only opportunity left available to him—that of pretending he was soon to become his son-in-law.

Tears of pain and betrayal welled in Ginny's eyes as the ache in her chest became intolerable. Her father had been used in the most callous way possible and she'd been a willing party to the injury.

Lifting one hand from the steering-wheel, she dropped her speed, rubbing her fist against the tense muscles in an abortive effort to ease them. How had she been so blind as not to suspect Steel's motives? He'd had nothing to lose. When Sullivan's went under, as it must do now, he could reclaim a good part of his investment from the sale of the existing stock, and doubtless Pandelis would reimburse him the remainder.

She was shivering now, oblivious of the voices which continued to sound in her ears. Steel must have seen his opportunity that first day, when he'd stormed into the office and seen the evidence of chaos all around him. Sharp businessman that he was, he'd realised the extent of Sullivan's vulnerability and taken instant advantage of it.

Not only the company's vulnerability, but her own. Last night he'd intended to use her the same way as he'd used Sullivan's: plundering, digesting and spitting out her bones when he was satisfied. Only the technicality of her virginity had stopped him in his tracks. What kind of man had she fallen in love with? she wondered distractedly. One who balked at seducing a virgin but could rape a company with no regrets?

Brushing the back of one hand against her tear-dampened lashes, she reached a decision. The war was over and Sullivan's had lost, but that wasn't going to prevent her from fighting one last battle. Face to face with Steel Anastasi she intended to make sure he'd be left in no doubt as to her opinion of him. Tough-skinned though he undoubtedly was, she'd mount a verbal assault on him which he'd remember for the rest of his unholy life! She'd take his precious *philotimo* and trample it into the ground!

Drawing in a deep breath, she forced herself to relax. The wheel of a car was no place for histrionics, but her decision was made. She'd continue northwards, direct into the heart of London. Once there she'd go to the Iliad Hotel and, if Steel wasn't there, she'd find out where he was. Nothing was going to rob her of her moment of confrontation.

Afterwards the drive to London was to remain lost forever in a haze at the back of her memory. But as she brought the Renault to a halt outside the Iliad and the doorman opened the impressive door of the luxury hotel for her, her courage nearly failed; then, as anger surged to sustain her, she marched up to the reception desk, her head held high.

'Will you please check if Mr Anastasi's in the penthouse suite?' she demanded briskly, proud of the way her voice came out cool and firm.

'Mr Anastasi is entertaining this evening,' the clerk told her suavely, his experienced eyes surveying the simple cream crinkle-cotton dress she'd chosen to wear for her excursion to the coast—one of her favourites, because with its V-necked sleeveless bodice and full skirt it was both cool and easy to wear, as well as being flattering to her long-legged, svelte figure.

'Excellent!' Deliberately she pretended to misunderstand him. 'I'll go straight up, then. I'm Ginette Sullivan, his fiancée. He's expecting me.' She moved swiftly in the direction of the lifts.

'Oh—Miss Sullivan—right!' Respect replaced indifference in the clerk's voice as Ginny reached her destination and pressed the button on the wall, smiling grimly to herself.

Charged now with a consuming fire of anger, she exited the lift to stride down the corridor. So Steel was entertaining! Whatever he'd provided to amuse his guests was going to pale into comparison with the fireworks she was about to let off! She planted her finger firmly on the bell outside his door and left it there.

She thought she was prepared for anything, but when the door was eventually opened by a beautiful blonde female who she guessed to be in her early to mid-thirties Ginny felt a shaft of pain so agonising she could hardly speak as jealousy seared a painful passage through her body, leaving in its trail the incredible knowledge that, despite everything he'd done, her love for Steel was not so easily aborted from her heart.

'I've come to see Steel.' Somehow she got the words out in response to the delicately raised eyebrows that challenged her. 'Perhaps you'll tell him I'm here.'

As the door was opened a little wider she accepted the invitation to enter, walking firmly over the threshold, noticing for the first time that the blonde was shoeless. Progressing further into the room, she observed a pair of spindly-heeled scarlet sandals lying abandoned on one of the pale rugs; rumpled cushions on the couch indicated where the woman had apparently been lying when the doorbell had aroused her with its urgent summons.

The room was empty of people, the entertaining Steel was doing limited to the one person. Where was he? she wondered. In the bedroom, preparing for or recovering from another conquest? Deliberately she ignored the

wave of the other woman's hand which invited her to be
seated.

She was conscious of pale blue eyes regarding her
speculatively as if aware of the torment she was valiantly
attempting to hide, before the blonde said quietly, 'He's
having a shower, but I'll tell him you're here.'

She didn't ask Ginny for her name, neither did Ginny
choose to volunteer it, the signs being that Steel's visitor
knew perfectly well who she was, either because the clerk
at the reception desk had phoned through before her
arrival, or more probably because Steel had already discussed her role in his life with his current paramour.
Instead she stood silently, watching the woman glide towards another door and disappear through its opening.

'Steel, darling...' The voice which drifted back was
low and melodious. 'Are you respectable? You've got a
visitor and I think she wants to see you urgently.'

There was a muffled exclamation from behind some
closed door, then the other woman was moving back
into the room with studied elegance, making her way to
the couch to retrieve and replace her sandals. 'He
shouldn't be long,' she observed calmly.

'Ginny! For the love of heaven. What's wrong?'

Steel burst into the room to stand there, barefooted,
naked from the waist up, light cotton trousers clinging
damply to his tautly muscled thighs. Dark hair clustered
in damp curls to his beautifully shaped head and Ginny
could even see droplets of water festooning his long eyelashes. His torso was unashamedly wet, the golden skin
gleaming in the diffused light of the room.

Releasing the rolled-up towel he'd been holding, allowing it to fall unheeded to the floor, he came towards
her, his arms outstretched as if to embrace her.

'No!' She almost screamed the word in her panic as she recoiled from his approach. 'Don't touch me!' Nothing had prepared her for the wave of emotion which engulfed her at the sight of him. What was happening to her? He was a monster, a criminal even—but she couldn't stop loving him...wanting him.

He stopped in mid-track, his face stilling with concern. 'Has something happened to Leo?'

'Were you expecting it to?' she laughed bitterly. 'No, my father's totally happy in his fool's paradise at the moment, making plans for a company that's going to be wiped off the face of the earth before the end of the week.'

A torrent of words which could only have been Greek obscenities burst from Steel's lips as an expression of anger replaced the previous concern which had masked his features.

A gentle cough reminded Ginny of their audience as Steel's previous visitor, having fastened her sandals, rose lazily to her feet to lay a soft hand on his naked arm.

'I'm obviously not wanted here at the moment,' she said softly, smiling up at him. 'Don't bother to see me out—I know my way.'

I bet you do, Ginny thought with untypical viciousness, unable to deny that she was breathtakingly lovely. Was she one of the women who would have been so hard to get rid of after a mock-engagement? she wondered.

'Hell, Stella...' Steel had the grace to look embarrassed. 'I'm sorry about this...' He gestured angrily towards Ginny as she stood, chin belligerently lifted, her eyes bright with recrimination. 'I wanted to...'

He didn't finish the sentence. Not that there was any need to. Ginny didn't have to be psychic to guess what Steel had wanted from a beautiful woman alone in his apartment in the early evening.

'Don't worry, darling.' Stella patted his arm. 'There'll be another opportunity—soon.'

'I hope so!' Steel bit out the words as Stella made her leisurely way towards the outer door, watching while she let herself out before turning his blazing regard on Ginny's accusing face.

'Now,' he commanded, a dark fury underlining the word and etching its presence on his autocratic face, 'you'd better tell me exactly what all this is about!'

'You've no idea, I suppose?' Ginny challenged vehemently, aware that she was shaking and that her voice betrayed her misery despite her effort to control it. 'I've come to congratulate you, of course. What a clever ploy it was to pretend to Dad that you and I were in love so you could gain the power to steal the Orchid franchise and then hand it over to Anastasi Holdings. Cleverer still to fool me into believing that you held some ancient grudge against Pandelis, so that I didn't question your eagerness to become Dad's partner too deeply!'

Adrenalin pumped through her blood, fuelling her determination for a final showdown. Like a forest fire her rage was intensifying, spreading through her body, flaming out through the power of speech, as Steel scowled at her with a dangerous intensity. 'Of course I always knew you had your own selfish interests at heart,' she went on bitterly. 'You made no secret of that! But I was too stupid to realise that Sullivan's would be a victim of them . . .

'Dad's a sick man!' Her voice broke, but she brought it instantly back under control. 'At this moment he's probably planning his future, totally unaware of the fact that you've handed his livelihood over to Anastasi Holdings.'

She was breathing heavily, watching Steel's heavy-lidded eyes, trying to estimate his reaction, wondering if he would have the grace to betray any remorse for the enormity of his sins, but he was standing rock-still, his face expressionless, as she made her final indictment. 'You called my father your friend. Tell me, what's the Hebrew translation of your name, Steel ... Judas?'

CHAPTER TWELVE

GINNY hadn't known what to expect, but Steel's immobility was almost as frightening as if he'd broken into violent abuse.

'So...what else have I been guilty of?' His softly voiced question broke the simmering tension building up between them. 'Or is that the end of your charges against me?'

'Don't mock me!' she flared back, her hands clenched with the effort of preventing them from lashing out at his supercilious face. 'What more is there? You took everything you wanted and left us all to rot!' Unmoved by his stony regard, she flung her head back, her grey eyes blazing their condemnation, and told the greatest lie of her life.

'I've come here to tell you I hate you, and I hope you go to hell!'

He moved as swiftly as a jungle cat which sensed the vulnerability of its prey, reaching out with purposeful hands to imprison her wrists, holding her helpless. 'You're right, *agape mou*.' His harsh laugh assailed her ears. 'I did take everything I wanted, but it was freely offered, and afterwards I tendered the highest price any man can offer for it—marriage.'

'Let me go!' His biting reminder did nothing to appease her. Fruitlessly she tried to free herself as the devilish gleam in his coal-black eyes told her he was controlling his temper by a slender margin. But the real pain was caused by the nearness and subtle scent of his warm, damp skin. He was her sworn enemy but, constrained against him, she was having difficulty in remembering that fact. 'I'd rather die than marry a man as ruthless as you! And you know perfectly well that's not what I'm talking about. Perhaps you were too occupied this afternoon to listen to the radio, but I heard everything—from Pandelis's own lips.' She fought fruitlessly against the power of his grip. 'Let me go!'

'Not before I show you exactly how ruthless I can be, Ginny.'

The face that stared down into her own was set in a mask of icy determination, the eyes dark and dangerous beneath heavy lids. Fear allied to anger giving her added strength, she made a renewed effort to escape, only to hear his contemptuous laugh as he changed his grasp to lift her clear of the ground, and she found her face forcibly buried in the warm flesh of his bare shoulder as he strode with her towards an inner door.

Seconds later she was released, dumped with little regard for her dignity on to a large double bed, while Steel remained standing over her, his breathing heavy, his hands splayed low on his hips. His muscular chest and arms gleamed with a patina of moisture, the ridged leanness of his abdomen advertised his fitness and his tan was a warm, deep gold against the closely tailored trousers that hugged the lines of his powerful male body with a faithful regard for its strength and litheness.

She had to get away! Wildly her eyes sought a means of escape, her agitated glance absorbing details of the room, observing that it must also serve as a study, since it contained a large desk and a built-in unit complete with hi-tech office equipment.

'Don't try anything, Ginny.' Husky and low, his voice told her he had anticipated her thoughts. 'If you value your beautiful skin, just stay where you are.'

Too proud to plead, she obeyed him, her mouth set in a mutinous line, her eyes bright with defiance as he strode towards the desk, to return immediately with three pieces of paper in his hand.

'Exhibit one,' he said tersely. 'A copy of the contract Leo signed this morning making me a full partner in Sullivan's. Exhibit two—a copy of the fax I sent to Orchid earlier, advising them that Sullivan's was on the threshold of considerable expansion, informing them that they could expect a large order within the week, and requesting confirmation that the existing franchise agreement would continue.'

Wordlessly, Ginny accepted the papers he thrust into her hands as he continued calmly, but with an edge to his voice which made the skin at the back of her neck tingle, 'Exhibit three—the reply I received back from them within the hour.'

Puzzled, she accepted the third sheet of paper and read the reply: 'Confirm validity of present franchise contract with Sullivan's—await your order with pleasure.'

The words swam before her eyes. 'You mean Sullivan's still has the sole distribution rights in this country?' she asked disbelievingly. 'But I heard your father...boasting that he'd bought control of Marsons and was introducing the Orchid range...' Her voice tailed away as Steel gave an exasperated sigh.

'So where's the problem?' he demanded. 'Sullivan's remains sole importer. Marsons buys direct from us at normal wholesale prices with the customary bulk discount. Not only do we have a new and very large customer, but by delivering direct from the docks to Anastasi Holdings' large London warehouse Sullivan's will have fulfilled its obligations to Orchid in a single stroke, increased its turnover by at least a hundred per cent and all that without incurring higher distribution or warehouse costs.'

'Oh!' Ginny swallowed painfully as her previous animosity drained, leaving her feeling weak and ill. It was all so devastatingly simple—and it had never occurred to her.

'*Oh*, indeed.' Steel's sensuous mouth snapped shut as he regarded her with obvious distaste. 'It was a shrewd business move which benefited all parties concerned. I didn't expect you to go down on your knees to me in gratitude, Ginny, but neither did I expect to be condemned to everlasting damnation.'

'I'm sorry.' Tribulation clouded her wide grey eyes as she forced them to scan his unforgiving face. Not that she deserved forgiveness. Nothing she could say would ever be enough to expiate her sins: the way she'd burst into his apartment, accused him of chicanery and spoiled the evening's entertainment he'd lined up for himself. 'Oh, Steel—I'm so dreadfully sorry!' She tried to scramble off the bed, her one intention to get out of his sight as quickly as she could. One thought alone comforted her. After her vicious display, Steel's imagined obligation to her would surely be in tatters. Not even a *philotimo* as powerful as his could demand that he marry a shrew—and a dim one at that.

'No, you don't!' He pushed her back again, standing towering over her. 'You can't storm in here, slander me before a witness and hope to escape without paying compensation.' He eased himself down beside her, cupped her anguished face in his hands and kissed her efficiently on her mouth. 'You owe me damages, Ginny, and by God you're going to pay them!'

'Steel, no!' Horrified as she read the intentions written plainly across his purposeful face, she tried to scramble away from him, resorting to a babble of words as her comparatively puny strength deserted her. 'I'm sorry...so dreadfully sorry about what I said—all the accusations I made. At the time it seemed so obvious...'

His face had gone very still, his eyes watchful, his mouth held in a straight line as she continued valiantly, 'Of course I'll do everything possible to put things right. I know you're furious about my bursting into your apartment, accusing you of duplicity and destroying the romantic evening you'd obviously planned to enjoy with Stella, but if you let me have her phone number I'll explain, apologise——'

'Stella!' Amazement and disbelief replaced the grimness on his face. 'Dear God, Ginny—what are you accusing me of now? Stella's my stepmother—Pandelis's wife! I had to collect her from Heathrow, because my father is still in Manchester reorganising the board at Marsons. In fact I left a message for you with Cathy explaining the situation and saying I'd be back later than I'd originally planned.'

Bewildered, Ginny shook her head, her mind only slowly assimilating what she'd just been told. 'I spent the afternoon at Worthing, then when I heard about Orchid on the car radio I came straight here,' she explained.

'And created an impression on my stepmother which is going to be very difficult to eradicate,' he told her dourly. 'Stella wanted to hear all about my fiancée and

I wanted to have a shower before going over to Taychapel to give you and Leo the good news about Orchid. So she made herself at home while I shouted out the answers to her questions from the sanctity of my bathroom. I planned to introduce you to her later this evening.' He heaved an exaggerated sigh. 'But as usual, *agape mou*, you did everything in your power to thwart me.'

'I'm only obstructive when your demands are unreasonable,' Ginny protested warily, relieved that he seemed to have regained his temper.

'I'm never unreasonable, Ginny.' The cynical amusement in his eyes exasperated her as he took her left hand and touched the circle of precious stones he'd placed there. 'One can't revitalise dying businesses by being unreasonable. Determined, perhaps.' He cast her a brooding glance. 'When I set my heart on something I don't give up easily. As you should know.'

'Which makes me one of several of my sex who can claim that knowledge, no doubt.' A small stab of pain pierced Ginny's heart as she tried to shrug off the inner emptiness she felt.

'You're jealous?' There was a new disturbing note in his voice.

'No, of course not!' She responded to the latent triumph in the question with a show of spirit, knowing she lied.

'Listen to me, Ginny.' His hand tightened around her cold fingers. 'There hadn't been any women in my life, let alone my bed, for a long time before I met you. It's not my habit to indulge in one-night stands or play the lover to disenchanted women who are bored with their own husbands. Recently I've been too busy chasing up business opportunities around the world to have time to form any kind of steady liaison——'

'Until Dad told you that anyone wanting a share of Sullivan's had to take Sullivan's daughter with it,' Ginny broke in bitterly.

'No,' he contradicted her calmly. 'Until Pandelis approached me with the prospect of taking Irene Stavrolakes as my wife...and I seriously considered doing just that.'

'But you said...' Perplexed, Ginny bit her lip, then lapsed into silence. What right did she have to cross-examine him?

'That I'd no intention of getting my father out of the trouble he well deserved to be in? Huh!' He gave a brief, sharp laugh. 'That was my first reaction. On the other hand Irene is a beautiful young woman, raised in the old-fashioned way to please the men in her family. She was willing for an alliance between us, and I had little doubt she'd make a dutiful and compliant wife and mother. In return I was prepared to be a faithful and considerate husband.' He shrugged. 'Many successful marriages have been founded on shakier bases than those.'

'But you felt nothing for her...' She paused, bewildered, as Steel shrugged impatiently.

'Love wasn't important to me. I'd learned all I needed to know about love from Louli!'

Flinching at the bitterness in his tone, Ginny shook her head sadly. 'You can't base your whole opinion of the female sex on one damning experience.'

'I could and I did,' he contradicted her flatly. 'Until the evening I stormed into Sullivan's yard determined to read the riot act—and discovered that the root of all the chaos was *you*, Ginny.' His gaze locked with hers for several seconds.

'I'd just flown back from Athens when Kostas phoned me in a state of great agitation to say that the Keys wouldn't be able to open for business that night because our true and trusted supplier had refused to deliver our order, which included vital lights, without advance payment. Can you imagine how I felt about that?'

She could—and did! Dumbly Ginny nodded as Steel's remorseless voice continued, 'I'd been intending to phone Pandelis to tell him I was prepared to consider his proposition. Instead I was obliged to drive over to Taychapel to find out what the hell was going on ... and there you were, the devoted daughter returned to the fold, inexperienced but enthusiastic, bent on a course of self-destruction and disaster.' His gaze narrowed reflectively. 'Not the most rewarding of meetings to begin with, *agape mou.*'

Irritated by the irony in his tone, Ginny rushed to defend herself. 'What did you expect?' she challenged. 'Dad was very ill, my holiday plans had collapsed, and you went out of your way to provoke me—dragging me up to London on a pretext which you later admitted was without foundation. I wasn't in the mood for celebration!'

'But you were in the mood for love,' he responded swiftly and softly. 'When the *ribetico* performer sang "How lonely, how desolate life is without love..." you sobbed out your despair in my arms.'

'No...' Steel was leading her down a dangerous path and she had to stop him before it was too late. 'How did I know what she was singing? I couldn't even translate the words,' she began desperately. 'I was tired——'

'And unhappy because the man you were going to marry had gone away without you.'

'He was a free agent,' Ginny protested desperately. 'I didn't blame him...'

'He was selfish and uncaring. He wasn't worthy to receive your love or your compassion, and when your body trembled in my arms I swore to myself that I'd take his place in your life before the summer ended.' Steel laughed softly. 'Somehow I'd teach you to love the things I loved, share my ambitions.' He made an expressive movement with his hands. 'Of course, at that time, I'd no idea how easy Leo was going to make it for me to become a part of your life, although I admit in the past he hadn't hidden from me his reservations about your schoolmaster friend——'

'He'd spoken that freely?' Ginny stared at him, biting her lip.

Steel shrugged. 'I told you we were friends and he was concerned for your happiness. Over a glass or two of ouzo I was a good listener.' He turned her palm and held it against his cheek, warming its coolness against his own vibrant flesh. 'I began to wonder what this daughter who embodied all the virtues of a paragon looked like, but the last photo her proud father could show me was taken when she was still at school.'

'I don't go in much for photographs.' She offered him a constrained smile, but he continued as if she hadn't spoken.

'Then six months ago I caught a glimpse of a girl in scarlet wool with a mop of unruly curls, and decided that when I had time to spare I'd make a point of asking her father to introduce us.'

Wearily, Ginny nodded. 'The catering fair,' she acknowledged dully. 'I must have made a big impression on you. You didn't recognise me when you stormed into the yard bent on retribution.'

'I told you, I had other things on my mind, and I'd only seen you at a distance. Besides, I wasn't expecting you to be there. Leo had already told me of your plans to holiday in Rome.'

'Well, it's no matter now.' Under his steady gaze, she shifted uneasily. 'You've accomplished everything you set out to do: make a business profit, frustrate your father and amuse yourself at my expense. I hope you've enjoyed the experience!'

'Oh, I have, Ginny.' He gave her a honeyed smile. 'Some parts of it more than others. On the whole it's been a very successful operation. Even Pandelis is coming to terms with not being able to link his name with Stavrolakes.'

'Since you offered him Orchid, no doubt!' She threw down the gauntlet, raising her direct gaze to interrogate him.

'That may have something to do with it,' he admitted, a dark fire flaring in the depths of his onyx eyes—a fire so openly erotic that Ginny tried to break away from him, tugging at her hand, but vainly as he used his free hand to gather her even closer. 'But more probably it's because of my recent betrothal.'

'To me?' Her voice rose an octave. 'But I thought...'

Steel grimaced. 'According to Stella, Pandelis's approval was absolutely genuine. It seems my beloved father was placing an each-way bet. He reckoned either

I'd agree to marry Irene to secure a seat on the board of Anastasi Holdings or, more probably, I'd be so incensed at the mere suggestion, I'd produce another bride. In either case he would have achieved what he *really* wanted—his itinerant son finally grounded as a responsible family man.'

Ginny closed her eyes in an attempt to hide her pain.

'So you won after all, Steel...' She swallowed hard to prevent the lump in her throat from choking her. 'We really fooled him, didn't we? What a laugh!'

She tried to smile but her lips quivered, and she had to turn her face away from him lest he see the signs of misery etched there.

'No, Ginny. I lost.' He spoke with such controlled anger that she swung her head back to look at him, marvelling at the sight of his face, nostrils flaring, mouth set in a grim line. 'When I lied to Leo about marrying you, it was with the best of intentions. I wanted to prevent his going bankrupt and I wanted to introduce you to new people and new events. Your father was so sure you were throwing yourself away on Howard, I thought I would be doing everyone a favour if I gave you the opportunity of standing away from your relationship with him—viewing your liaison from a distance.'

'You certainly did that,' she murmured, transfixed by the dark beauty of his anguished face, the harsh undertones of his voice.

'And fell into my own trap,' he returned bitterly. 'By interfering with your relationship with Howard I strengthened your love for him. By making you lie to him I earned only your hate, by seducing you—*theos mou*!' His voice broke. 'I took from you the gift you'd saved for the man you were about to marry...'

'Oh, Steel, it wasn't like that!' Horrified at the remorse which engraved lines of pain on his handsome face, Ginny flung her arms round him, abandoning all pride. 'I wanted you. I wanted you so much!'

'But I *love* you, Ginny,' he said simply. 'That's the difference. I love you and I wanted to marry you. I really believed from everything I'd heard from Leo, and your own reaction to me in the Keys, that whatever you and Howard felt for each other it wasn't enough.'

A wry, self-mocking smile turned the corners of his mouth. 'I still believe that, Ginny. The only difference now is I realise I'm not what you want either. Indifference I could have worked on to change, but hate? No, Ginny, your hate has defeated me.'

Love? He had said he loved her? He'd said a number of other things but she'd barely registered them.

'Wh-what did you say?' She reared away from him like a startled filly.

'That I gambled and lost. I'll tell Leo everything...'

'No, no!' She was trembling now. 'You said something about loving me!'

'Amusing, isn't it?' His bark of laughter was forced and harsh. 'I'd imagined myself immune to such an emotion, but Leo did such an excellent public relations job on your behalf, I was probably half in love with his generous, open-hearted, compassionate daughter even before I met her.'

She *had* heard him aright. He didn't have to repeat the magic phrase. It was seared on her memory, and every tortured line of his face confirmed it. A wild, vibrant joy sang through Ginny's blood. Steel Anastasi loved her.

'You disguised it well!' Still hardly able to believe her ears, she hid her tumultuous feelings, hugging her pleasure to herself, teasing him just a little to test her new-found power.

'I didn't want to believe it.' He held her hand against his chest so that her palm registered the thunder of his heart. His eyes were slumbrous, heavy with desire. 'I'd trodden that path once before—or thought I had—when I was a teenager. Love wasn't part of my plans for the future. But when I walked into Sullivan's yard and discovered you, fighting to save the business like a tigress protecting her young, I knew I couldn't walk away and leave you. I told myself I was intervening solely because of Leo, but instinctively I knew it was more than that.'

His dark features were taut, unrelenting as he held her unwavering gaze. 'As God is my judge, Ginny, I meant to take things slowly, but I miscalculated the strength of my own feelings, the extent of my own self-control. Then when I discovered I was your first lover it was too late for finesse...'

'Because honourable men don't seduce their friends' daughters?' she chided gently.

'Because I knew I loved you,' he corrected her quietly. 'And time had run out on me.'

'Oh, Steel...' she began, her eyes ablaze with happiness, only to find that he was no longer looking at her, but staring into space.

'It's all right, Ginny. I know when I'm beaten. I mean to tell Leo the truth—everything. How I blackmailed you into——'

'You most certainly will not!'

Her sharp interjection caused his head to jerk back in astonishment.

'How dare you suggest such a thing?' she continued to admonish him, stifling her amusement at the blankness of his expression. 'You come into my life, lie to everybody in sight, open my eyes to the fact that I was about to marry a man I didn't love, introduce me to your father, have your evil way with me and then think you can walk out of my life! And worse, far worse than all those things put together...' She paused to gaze into his face. It was still, frozen like that of a statue, the eyes expectant, the mouth set firm. She heaved in a great breath to sustain herself. 'Worst of all, Steel Anastasi, you made me fall in love with you, and I'm afraid I'm going to insist on marriage.'

He didn't speak, but his face told her everything as he reached for her, his arms tightening convulsively around her as he bent his glossy head, his hard mouth seeking the softness of her eagerly offered lips in a violent, passionate act of possession, and Ginny shuddered as the persuasion of his mouth awakened a surge of response that filtered through her entire body.

Suddenly she was gasping helplessly as a rising tide of excitement trembled through her limbs, heightening her senses so that everything in the room was sharper, the air more scented, Steel's own aura so vibrantly pervasive that she felt she was caught in a growing fount of joy, spiralling ever upwards.

She was experiencing a bewildering happiness that she'd never dreamed existed. It was both alarming and awe-inspiring, like an orgasm of the spirit. Perhaps the depth of Steel's kiss was depriving her of oxygen? she wondered faintly. Yes, that must be it! As his lips released her, she struggled weakly against him, able at last to voice her fears.

'I feel—I feel so very strange...' And then, without his having to speak a word, she knew; she remembered his voice, serious and controlled, saying, 'It can't be bought or forced and some people never know it in a lifetime. But to be possessed by *kefi* is to know that life is for living joyfully, is to be a free spirit at one with the ancient gods...'

'Yes, *agape mou*,' Steel whispered against her hair, strong hands holding her steady against his powerful frame. She could feel his body taut with desire, feel his heartbeart like a drum against the softness of her breasts as his hands moved with stunning tenderness against the thin material which concealed her body from his eyes, arousing its dormant hunger. 'I feel it too. The gods have given us their blessing.'

The arms which had been comforting became more urgently possessive as he felt her soft body speak its silent need against him. 'Tell me, Ginny, will you mind very much exchanging a holiday in Rome for a honeymoon in the Greek islands?' he murmured against her cheek.

'Why else do you suppose I'm going to marry you?' she asked in mock-surprise. 'Although...' Even in the throes of passion, her sensitive conscience twinged. 'I know it's a lot to ask, but do you think we could defer it until Dad's fully recovered? I don't really like to leave him alone.'

'What makes you think he'll be alone?' Steel kissed the concern from her anxious face. 'Don't you remember my telling you that Cathy was looking forward to getting married?'

'Cathy!' Ginny's jaw dropped. 'You mean Cathy and Dad...?'

Steel nodded his sleek, dark head. 'He put off telling you, Ginny. He didn't know how you would take to the idea of having a stepmother after all these years.'

'I couldn't be happier!' She frowned as a thought crossed her mind. 'Do you mind dreadfully that your father is pleased about us?'

'How can I?' He gave her a wry smile. 'Besides, Pandelis and I understand each other. The friction between us creates a heat which warms as well as scorches on occasion. With you as mediator, who knows? We may even become friends in the future. Must we discuss him now?'

'Of course not.' Lying back on the pillows, she opened her arms wide to receive him.

If the first time they'd become lovers had been memorable, then the second was indescribable. But the Greeks would have a word for it—they always did. Later, much later, she would ask Steel what it was. For now it was sufficient to enjoy it.

Harlequin Romance ®

brings you

How the West was Wooed!

We've rounded up twelve of our most popular authors, and the result is a whole year of romance, Western style. Every month we'll be bringing you a spirited, independent woman whose heart is about to be lassoed by a rugged, handsome, one-hundred-percent cowboy! Watch for...

- March: **CLANTON'S WOMAN**—Patricia Knoll

- April: **A DANGEROUS MAGIC**—Patricia Wilson

- May: **THE BADLANDS BRIDE**—Rebecca Winters

- June: **RUNAWAY WEDDING**—Ruth Jean Dale

- July: **A RANCH, A RING AND EVERYTHING**—Val Daniels

HITCH-2

Harlequin Romance ®

brings you

Some men are worth waiting for!

They're handsome, they're charming but, best of all,
they're single! Twelve lucky women are about to
discover that finding Mr. Right is not a problem—it's
holding on to him.

In March the series continues with

#3401 THE ONLY MAN FOR MAGGIE
by Leigh Michaels

Karr Elliot wanted Maggie off his property but not out
of his life. But Maggie didn't want a man—she wanted
her own apartment!

Hold out for Harlequin Romance's heroes in
coming months...

- April: **THE RIGHT KIND OF MAN**—Jessica Hart

- May: **MOVING IN WITH ADAM**—Jeanne Allan

- June: **THE PARENT TRAP**—Leigh Michaels

UNLOCK THE DOOR TO GREAT ROMANCE AT BRIDE'S BAY RESORT

Join Harlequin's new across-the-lines series, set in an exclusive hotel on an island off the coast of South Carolina.

Seven of your favorite authors will bring you exciting stories about fascinating heroes and heroines discovering love at Bride's Bay Resort.

Look for these fabulous stories coming to a store near you beginning in January 1996.

Harlequin American Romance #613 in January
Matchmaking Baby by Cathy Gillen Thacker

Harlequin Presents #1794 in February
Indiscretions by Robyn Donald

Harlequin Intrigue #362 in March
Love and Lies by Dawn Stewardson

Harlequin Romance #3404 in April
Make Believe Engagement by Day Leclaire

Harlequin Temptation #588 in May
Stranger in the Night by Roseanne Williams

Harlequin Superromance #695 in June
Married to a Stranger by Connie Bennett

Harlequin Historicals #324 in July
Dulcie's Gift by Ruth Langan

Visit Bride's Bay Resort each month wherever Harlequin books are sold.

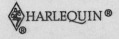

BBAYG